Love, Your Fangirl

A Novel

JESSICA EISSFELDT

Love, Your Fangirl: A novel
Jessica Eissfeldt

Copyright © 2014 by Jessica Eissfeldt. All rights reserved.
First published April 2020.
Print Edition

ISBN: 978-1-989290-10-1

Also By Jessica Eissfeldt

Sweet Historical Romance

Sweethearts & Jazz Nights
Dialing Dreams
Shattered Melodies
Fancy Footwork
Unspoken Lyrics
The Sweethearts & Jazz Nights Boxed Set: The Complete Collection

Love By Moonlight
Beneath A Venetian Moon
Besides A Moonlit Shore
The Love By Moonlight Boxed Set: The Complete Collection

Sweet Contemporary Romance

Prince Edward Island Love Letters & Legends
This Time It's Forever
Now It's For Always
At Last It's True Love

Romance Collections

Love & Lattes: A Sweet Romance Short Story Collection

Chick Lit

Love, Your Fangirl

Dear Reader,

This novel languished in the proverbial shoebox for years before I decided to take it to press.

Deciding to publish this novel was a risk for me because, as I read back through this story, there are places I now see that could be changed or modified, thanks to the writing experience I've gained since I wrote it.

But I've decided to change nothing and leave it as-is because, at the time, I sincerely believed it was the best story I could write.

Today, I still believe in the message and the themes this story conveys. So I've chosen to publish it.

With that in mind, I humbly extend this gift of writing to you, the reader. I hope you enjoy it, just as it was written.

Happy reading!
J.E.
April 2020

Chapter One

U M, YEAH. I'M not supposed to be here. Well, technically, that's not true. It's perfectly fine to be in the shopping district of downtown Regina at 11 a.m. on a Saturday morning; unless, of course, you're running way late for your cousin's surprise birthday luncheon—that you're supposed to be hosting on a shoestring budget. Which I am.

I sigh. I thought that by twenty-four, I'd have it all together: the great job, the great guy... the great hair.

Okay, so maybe having all that by twenty-four is a tad unrealistic, but great hair would be nice, at least. I push those thoughts, along with my unruly curls, away from my forehead and push my glasses up the bridge of my nose.

Well, at least it's a gorgeous November day. (No snow! Above freezing!) So I drive a little faster and crank up my favorite Taylor Swift song, singing along off-key. But thanks to those singing lessons I took last year, I'm actually *almost* on-pitch.

Yep. Nothing could burst my bubble.

Until I hear an actual pop.

Getting to places on time would be nice, too. But life, the universe, whatever you want to call it, well, it clearly has a different plan for me than what I'd seen in my Tarot cards earlier this morning.

I pull up to the curb and get out. The car looks

fine... Front driver's wheel—check. Front passenger wheel—check. Rear passenger wheel—check. Rear driver's...Oh crap. It's totally flat.

No problem. Easy fix. I turn on my phone. Yep, this will *all* be fine.

Until it isn't.

Because an angry ding tells me my phone has just died.

I glance around, half expecting to see the solution to my problem pop up out of thin air. And then it does. I see the sign for Arthur's Antiques. I love antique stores. Was it mere coincidence I got a flat here? I think not.

The bell jingles as I open the door.

"Looking for anything in particular?"

"A telephone."

"Sure, we got lots of them. Which era?"

"Modern. I need to call CAA and get a flat fixed."

"Sure, just over at the counter."

I wander through the aisles toward the counter and inhale that delicious combination of musty books and faded memories. Antique stores give me hope. Hope that maybe I can learn from my past mistakes to create a better future—a future that includes a man who truly loves me. Hope that the most important things in life—love, laughter, and friendship—never really fade away, but keep living on, passed down through multiple generations.

Like in books, for example. I trail a finger across the gilt-edged spines of the dusty volumes and sigh. Too bad I can't just use someone else's words to ease my writer's block. Ugh. My stupid ex-boyfriend—it was his fault I had writer's block to begin with.

But I can't blame him anymore, really. It was my own decision to stay with him for that long, but my inner writer hasn't recovered from the wounds he inflicted.

I'm just about to reach the counter when the corner of an old LP catches my eye. Oooh, I've been looking for more records to add to my collection. Is it a 45 or a 78?

I pick it up and blow off the thick layer of dust. A 45. Perfect fit for my player. I've never heard of the singer, though—Tom White.

I study the distinctive 1940s lettering on the cover, then ease it off to read the liner notes. Oh. My heart beats a little faster. It's jazz. I love jazz. I glance at the black and white photo, my eyes drawn to the man's expression, alight with joy.

Tom White was *definitely* handsome. A shiver slides down my spine—but that's just because it's just cold in here. It has nothing to do with the fact that his face seems somehow...familiar.

I roll my eyes at myself. His face can't be familiar. That's just ridiculous. One of my romantic, flyaway notions. But I still plunk down the album on the countertop. "I'll take this, thanks." Gotta thank the guy for letting me use his phone, right?

✧ ✧ ✧

THAT EVENING, I head back to the apartment I share with my best friend Cerise.

I let myself in and shut the door behind me.

"Hey, Vicky," Cerise shouts over the clatter and bang of baking tins. She must be making her famous man-catcher muffins again. I wonder who the hapless male du jour is. "How'd the surprise party go?"

"Let's just say I got more than I bargained for." I hold up the record and poke my head into the kitchen. Yep. She's holding a cup of raspberries. "Who's your next victim?"

The pink streak in her jet-black ponytail bobs as she laughs at my teasing. "You know, this might do you some good, too." She pours the raspberries into the bowl and folds them into the batter before scooping it into the muffin tins.

"What, baking? You know I hate it."

"Man-catching. Er, dating." She puts the tins into the oven. "You haven't had a date in—"

"Four years. I know." I take a step back, straddling the threshold between the kitchen and living room.

Her tone softens. "They're not all Jason, you know."

"You're dripping batter onto the floor."

"Don't change the subject." She puts the spatula back into the empty bowl in the sink.

"Too late." I swipe a taste of the remaining batter. "Mmmm, delicious as always. Anyway, you're gonna be late if you don't go now."

She surveys the mountain of dishes before glancing at her watch.

"Don't worry, I'll do them. I'm going to have a relaxing evening in, anyway. Maybe a nice hot bubble bath. Eat too many muffins and cuddle up with Sinatra."

"Crap. That's what I forgot. He's still locked in the bathroom. Didn't want him to jump onto the counter and get cat hair in the batter."

"I'll let him out. I'm on my way to my room anyway."

"Thanks."

After she leaves, the apartment is too quiet. I open the bathroom door and a black and white streak darts out, then winds around my legs. I bend down to stroke his fur and am rewarded with a loud, rumbling purr. "What would I do without my jazz man?" Sinatra butts his head against my hand and purrs louder. He starts to follow me into my bedroom, but I shut the door before he can.

Cerise's words follow me; my grip tightens on the record. Four years is way too long to be single, but I can't help it. I clench my jaw. I know men are not all abusive manipulators like Jason but... No. I'm not going to ruin my night by thinking about my past. So I slip the vinyl record out of the case and onto the turntable.

Tom White's voice washes over me, mellow and soothing, cleansing away every last bit of fear and doubt as he croons about the promise of everlasting love and the beauty of romance. A magical place where men are good and faithful to the women they love.

I brush away a tear and sit up, my heart beating in time with the tempo; the crackles and pops of the record making me smile. Now *this* is how music is supposed to sound. Real. (Plus, it's a great excuse to forget about my writer's block and lack of a love life.)

A few minutes later, I'm sound asleep.

❖ ❖ ❖

HIS HANDS CRADLE *the microphone like a lover's face, his voice caresses each note, the spotlight shining on the Brylcreem in his jet-black hair. The look in his hazel eyes as he gazes out into the audience seems tailor-made for me.*

Because it is.

The corners of my mouth lift up into a secret smile—he is mine. Now and always. I can feel the still-unfamiliar weight of the engagement ring on my finger. My heart beats so fast through the thin crepe silk of my best dress that I fear it might take flight.

The final notes fade away and the audience jumps to its feet, the applause deafening, whistles and catcalls all around.

I dart through the crowd and dash backstage to his dressing room.

I slip inside and have just enough time to touch up my lipstick before the door opens. He pulls me to him, stroking my hair. "Oh, darling. I don't want to wait any longer."

"You mean that?"

"Yes, darling, yes, I do. I don't care what any of the other fellows think."

"But I thought you said George...I mean, with the tour, and your new album..."

"Blast all of that." He kisses my eyes, my hair, my lips. "I love you. The only thing that matters right now is being together. Let's get married tonight."

✧ ✧ ✧

THE BLARE OF my alarm jolts me awake. I stretch and blink sleepily. That was one heck of a realistic dream.

I bring a hand up to my mouth. I can almost feel the touch of that man's lips on mine...

I reach for my almost-full dream journal, which is balanced precariously on top of my well-thumbed dream dictionary. I scribble down the details of this latest dream and then glance at the clock. 6 a.m.

Full of resolve to actually get some words down on paper, I pick up my Mac.

Hmmm, I wonder if Sinatra needs to be brushed. He *is* shedding. Or maybe I could do some laundry? No. No. Focus. Write. I put my fingers on the keyboard. Or, wait. How about, I don't know, washing the floor?

I force myself to stay seated.

The cursor hovers over Microsoft Word, but my eyes flick to the Internet browser instead. I know. I'll check my email. Just a quick peek before I get started on a new story. I click the web browser open.

Ooo, a new email. It's from Cerise. Oh, this'll only take a minute. Then I'll start writing.

> *Hey girl! Found this cute Toronto jazz singer for you. Check out his music video on his website: www.ericblackjazz.com.*

Hey, this is like a little pre-writing break. Just five minutes... My eyes flick to the clock.

Crap! I need to hurry it up or I'm going to be late for work. Eric Black's website will have to wait.

I jump up out of bed, whip off my pajamas covered in black-and-white cat hair, toss on a fresh T-shirt and pair of jeans, run a brush through my curls, and grab my purse. It's only then that I realize the record player is still playing.

✧　✧　✧

I NEEDN'T HAVE rushed. No one's around on a chilly Sunday morning. I shiver and step into a patch of sunlight that streams through the bookstore windows, warming my shoulders, and the aroma of coffee from the in-store café drifts past my nose. Mmmmm. I feel myself start to get a bit drowsy as I absently start to remove a poster from the front door.

I shake off the feeling as I see a man approach. A very *hot* man, I might add. My palms start to sweat and my shoulders tense even after I see there's a tentative look on his face.

"Excuse me. I'm looking for a birthday present for my wife."

Oh, thank God he's not single. The tension in my neck relaxes.

"She loves classic novels and has read so many of them... I want to surprise her, and there's one author she hasn't read that I think she'd like. The name starts with a J..." He squints at me as if expecting me to know the answer.

Which, technically, I should know. I mean, I work here. But I'm not a mind reader. Still, I try.

"A 'J', you say? Hmmm. How about Jane Austen? Or there's Joseph Conrad. Or John Steinbeck. John Grisham—but he's probably too modern. Plus, he writes about lawyers, which aren't exactly classic subject matter. Of course, then again, there's always Mark Twain or Charles Dickens if you're looking for..." I see the man's blank expression.

"Sorry." I laugh. "Got a bit carried away. Right. Classics." I start walking toward the classic literature section, continuing to talk as I walk. All the while wishing that it was *my* book that someone had come in to ask about.

We reach the stacks and I point to the A's. "Jane Austen's always a good bet. I recommend *Persuasion*."

"No, no. I know it wasn't Jane Austen." He squints again and shakes his head. "Now I remember! The author's name is Jane Eyre."

"Jane Eyre? She's not—"

But he cuts me off. "Yes." He nods again, completely sure of himself.

I feel a twinge of indignation but shove it back down. I have to be polite. Friendly. Knowledgeable. (It's in my contract.) Besides, if there's one thing I'm sure about, it's book titles and characters.

"Jane Eyre was a character. Not an author. Charlotte Brontë wrote the book."

"Are you sure?"

"Positive. *Jane Eyre* is the book's title, not the author." I reach down, pull it off the shelf, and hand it to him.

His eyes light up and I feel a twinge of sadness. I wish it was my book making someone that happy.

After the customer leaves, I walk through the aisles trying to look busy as I fight off boredom. I dust shelves. Straighten books.

Just then, my boss appears, waving a torn poster. "Did you do this?" he says without preamble.

"I took it off the front doors, if that's what you mean. Just like you asked me to."

He shoves it under my nose. "We can't have this kind of carelessness in my bookstore. There's still tape stuck to the doors." He shakes his head.

"But right in the middle of taking down the poster, there was a customer who asked me for—"

"Do it right next time *before* you run off to help customers."

I open my mouth to protest, to stand up for myself; to do something. But in the end I just fake a smile and nod at him. I need the rent money. "It won't happen again."

He walks away and I return to front doors to take off the bits of tape.

The glow of the morning sun makes the book covers shine. And I can't help myself. I trail a finger along the books; the bumpy raised lettering of the titles, the scent of new ink, the smooth slide of glossy paper all comfort me.

I inhale and feel myself relaxing. All these books. All these authors. I smile. I'm among friends, just like Emerson said. And all these authors made their dreams come true, didn't they?

I gaze up at the bestseller wall. My imagination takes over as I see my own novel among those titles. Now if only I could actually *write* one.

❖ ❖ ❖

I GET BACK home and, after I feed Sinatra, I head to my laptop. Oh yeah. Now I have time and I can check out that jazz singer's website. I click the link.

Oh my God.

Sunlight streams through his wavy brown hair as he lies on the lawn. The green grass offsets his navy-blue button-down shirt in just the right way, a way that makes me want to touch it, touch him...

I squeeze my eyes shut. No. No. No. I'm not going there. No. This is just a video. This is *not* real. Not real. Breathe in. Breathe out. I will not get caught up.

But desire and longing surge through me without warning. (Four years *is* a long time without a boyfriend, after all.) As if they have a mind of their own, my fingers slowly, slowly move toward him, toward the light, toward that beautiful, beautiful scene. My fingers itch to feel the smooth cotton chambray of his shirt, feel the prickly softness of the grass, feel the warm sun against my skin as both of us are bathed in the glow of the late summer sun.

Thankfully, my fingers bounce back against the firm barrier of the laptop screen. (Damn it. Apple's hi-res display makes this seem way too real.)

I sigh and rub my fingers, wishing I could rub away the longing in my heart.

He looks so happy. And suddenly, I'm envious of the woman in the video who's pretending to be his girlfriend. Envious of that fake camaraderie and that fake flower he's given her, tucked into her blonde hair. She looks so happy.

And for a moment, the music makes me forget.

Forget everything that is so out of reach for me right now. Forget my lack of a love life. Forget that I'm working a crappy retail job for $9.75 per hour, despite the fact that I have a degree in creative writing. No. I'm not going to think depressing thoughts.

Hmmmm. What are the rest of his songs like? I click on the button that lets me stream the rest of his latest album.

I sigh with pleasure this time, allowing myself to

get carried away...just drifting and floating along, the smooth, easy melody washing through me.

All at once, I feel tears building. Brimming. Spilling over. Now they're streaming down my face. And I'm sobbing uncontrollably. Big, deep, racking sobs, as if my heart is breaking.

As if my heart has already shattered into a thousand pieces, ones that are so small and so fragile that nothing in the world can put them back together again.

I cock my head. This song...

Wait. Wait. I wipe away the tears. This is the song that was on Tom White's record. I frown.

And all at once, I can see it. My heart beats faster and my eyes widen. Could it be?

Yes. Yes. Images are falling into place in my mind. Images part of, and yet not part of the song's lyrics. Images that intermingle with pictures from my dream. A crowded dance floor. Bobby pins. The blare of saxophone and trumpet.

And now I hear it—snatches of dialog. And the images keep coming.

So I start typing.

Chapter Two

GOD. I LOVE this! I've been at it for a few days and already I have more pages than I thought possible. And a really stiff neck, from hunching over the keyboard, but hey, I don't really care because I have one hundred and fifty pages inspired by Eric Black.

He totally saved me. Saved my writing career. (Well, okay, that might be a bit of wild exaggeration. But wild exaggeration is, like, my middle name.)

"I thought you had writer's block?" Cerise blinks sleepily, toothbrush in hand.

I look up at her and laugh. "That's over. It's easy now. And it's all because of Eric Black. I never knew it could be like this. I mean, wow. I don't even know *where* this inspiration is coming from, but right after I heard Eric's song, this stuff just hasn't stopped."

She rubs her eyes. "You're playing jazz at 5 a.m."

"I can turn down the volume if you want."

"Uh, Vicky, that's not the point. Don't you think this pace is unhealthy?"

I blink, my fingers suspended for a second over the keys. "I don't have time to psychoanalyze right now. My characters are calling." I grin, turn my head back to the laptop and type faster, the mellow croon of Eric's voice filling my head.

❖ ❖ ❖

MORNING AFTER MORNING, I show up at the keyboard. My story even has a title now—*Lyrics of Love*. I can't seem to stop writing.

Eric's voice swirls around me. Images fill my mind as his music fills my heart.

I close my eyes. To listen. To watch. More pieces of the story unfold inside me. And so I surrender.

The hero and heroine are in a smoky bar and it's dark and the music's so loud and I can almost feel the burn of gin in my throat as the heroine downs a glass, her toes tapping to the furious beat of the bass violins and—ahhhhh! I can't take this.

But my fingers, instead of lifting from the keyboard, fly even faster. I realize I'm sweating.

I'm totally lost. Lost within the world of the characters, their hopes and fears, and it's all I can do to keep up with it. *God*. This feels so *real*. I gasp for breath as the lazy melody of Eric's voice weaves its way deeper into me even as I dig deeper into the story.

It feels like...*home*, I realize. I'm not lost. I'm coming home. To the keyboard, to the voices and visions, to the power of the words churning through me, the unfolding story. All of it. Home to myself. Home to my passion. Home to my heart.

And through it all, Eric keeps singing.

❖ ❖ ❖

CERISE POKES HER head around my door. "Oh hey, you're still alive." She pulls something out of her purse. "Just checked the mailbox. This came for you."

I blink and look over at her. "What's that?"

She glances at the return address. "Ticketmaster, looks like. Must be those Taylor Swift concert tickets you bought." She puts the envelope on the edge of the desk and then walks back toward the door.

"Oh, and guess what?"

"What?" I reach for the envelope. *Taylor Swift, here I come.*

"Eric Black is coming to the casino for a show on May."

I drop the envelope. "Really?"

She grins. "So I bought us two tickets. Early birthday present."

I jump up and practically break her ribs with my hug.

"Don't kill me yet." She gasps between laughs. "I still have to prep my poetry reading for tonight." Her face drops. "Maybe a local audience will like it better than that stupid literary magazine. They rejected me. *Again.* Now I'll never be a published poet."

"Cerise, think logically. It's only one magazine. I'm not trying to be unsympathetic here, but even if they did reject you, you'll get another chance with a different magazine. It's not the end of the world."

"That's a shocking bit of logic coming from you, Miss Crazy Illogical."

I give her a playful shove. "I like to think I have at least a toe on logical ground, you know."

"Thanks for the pep talk. And you're welcome for the tickets." She pauses in the doorway. "By the way, they're VIP."

THE NEXT MORNING, after furiously writing for forty-five solid minutes, I head to my room to get ready for work. (Don't want to be late.) But I pause in the hall to feed Cerise's goldfish, Plato He swims slowly to the surface of the fish tank. Hmmmm.

I don't have time to contemplate what might or might not be wrong with her fish because the phone rings. It's my boss. "Yeah, I'm on my way now. Sorry about that. I—"

I pull the phone away from my ear as he starts yelling. (Why do I work for him again? It's probably because of the forty percent discount on books that I get.)

As I get into my Focus and drive to the bookstore, a sense of unease creeps over me. How did I go from feeling so frustrated, angry and scared about writing to having such a strong, frenzied urge to write?

Is some sort of universal energy helping me out here? But then again, something about this feels too easy.

✧ ✧ ✧

AT WORK, I'M rearranging the stack of community newspapers by the door, my mind still focused on my hero and heroine, when I see the headline:

2013 Jegg Awards Coming to Regina: Volunteers Wanted

I glance around. No supervisor in sight.

So I pick up the paper and skim the article. Album of the year nominees, artist of the year nominees… Wow. Taylor Swift's latest album is nominated. And

Michael Bublé's hosting. Whoa.

Canada's equivalent of the Grammy Awards is coming here! A sly grin creeps across my face. This could be fun.

Just then, I feel a tap on my shoulder.

"Vicky." It's my boss standing there with his arms crossed.

I swallow. Put down the paper. "Yes?"

"We need to talk. Come with me."

I follow him to his office. "Vicky, this isn't working out. You've been showing up late for quite a few days in a row now. And you have a tendency to daydream when you should be helping customers. I'm going to have to let you go."

I look at him, heart beating fast, slow grin spreading across my face. "Really?"

"Yes."

I feel like tap dancing on the desk.

Yes. I'm free at last! Bye-bye, boss from hell. Hello, more writing time.

❖   ❖   ❖

THAT SAME NIGHT, as I walk into the kitchen to make myself some tea, it hits me. How am I going to pay the rent? My bills? I don't have much money saved. It'll get me by for a few months, I guess... I shove those thoughts aside as I spot Cerise leaning against the counter, spatula in one hand, mixing bowl sitting abandoned on the counter.

"Cerise, what's wrong?"

"My date went so well the other night." She puts down the spatula and takes a seat at the table. "But then he never called me back even after he *said* he would."

She picks up what looks like a mug of cold coffee. "My car just got rear-ended. And now, to top it all off, Plato's *dead*." Cerise stares into her coffee, absently stirring it round and round. I can't help but notice the cream she'd poured in it swirls into vaguely fish-like shapes.

I put a hand on her arm. "I'm sorry, Cerise. About the date. Your car. And about Plato."

"I know it's ridiculous. Plato was my goldfish, not a person. And I know I'll find another date. So why am I so upset about it?"

"I get what you're feeling right now because well, um, I just got fired today. I mean, I have a bit of savings for a little while so I can still pay my half of the rent and utilities but like, I know what you mean."

She chews on the tiny black plastic coffee stirrer and looks at me as if I have all the answers in the world.

If only. So I don't say anything, just let her go on.

"I just...ugh. I got up this morning and he was just floating there...his little body bobbing on the surface, his tail at a crooked angle and I felt this awful, horrible jolt run through me. I just...It feels like it's my fault. Crazy, right?" She crushes the stirrer between her fingers, and I wish I could find a way out of this blame trap that she's put herself in.

"He's just a goldfish." She shakes her head. "But some part of me feels like it's the whole law of attraction thing! I thought it, and it came true, so of course it's all my fault. I totally brought it upon myself, and since you know as well as I do that we're all empowered—"

"We're all empowered to choose how we feel, too, you know."

She crosses her arms.

"And blaming yourself is not going to help anything now." I swirl the dregs of my drink around in my cup.

"Yeah, maybe you're right." I can tell she doesn't believe me. "I know, I know. I'm whining. I know I sound like I'm five years old. Ugh. It just really reminded me of my own mortality, I guess."

"Well, who knows? Maybe some hypnotherapy or a past-life regression would help you figure out the root issue here. I mean, I did a past-life regression last month when I was going through some issues about my mom and now things are better between us." I pause and look at her.

"Hmmm. I could do that. I mean, there's so much I haven't done, so much I want to do... and that scares me. Or, hey," She sits up straighter. "Maybe this is like, a wake-up call, or a sign. You know what, Vicky? That's exactly it. I'm going to make a bucket list."

I put my cup down with a firm clink, feeling a renewed sense of strength flow through me. "You know what? That's a great idea. I'm totally going to make one too. I'm going to do something I've always wanted to do. I'm not going to be afraid anymore. No. I'm going to do something...*awesome*. I'm going to volunteer for the Jeggs!"

❖ ❖ ❖

"LET ME REPEAT—THERE will be *no* asking for photo-

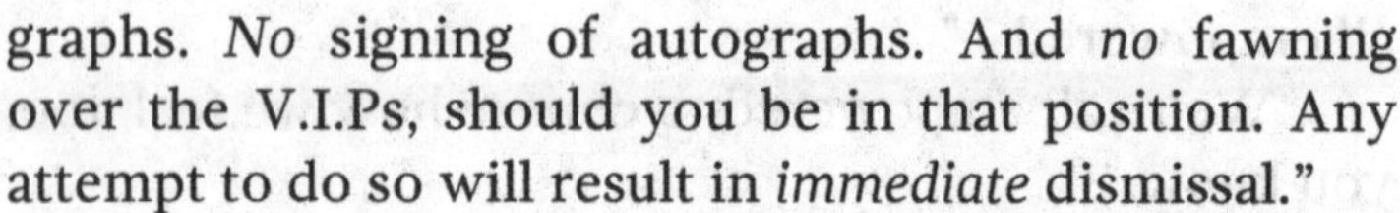

graphs. *No* signing of autographs. And *no* fawning over the V.I.Ps, should you be in that position. Any attempt to do so will result in *immediate* dismissal."

Whew. For a second there I thought he was going to say execution.

As the bald man stands on the stage at the Brandt Center and glares out into the audience, I swallow.

He pounds the lectern. "There will be *no* accepting of gratuities. *No* gifts. *No* favors."

I press back into my seat.

"Sounds like someone could really use a laugh," Cerise whispers to me as frowny-face continues talking.

Now he's pointing to a PowerPoint slide about our uniforms. Black slacks. White button-down dress shirt. And of course, highly polished black shoes. And the requisite volunteer vest, with the Jegg Awards logo on it—that looks, I realize, sort of like a grain elevator. (Makes sense, actually, since this province is responsible for more than half the country's grain production.)

I mean, okay, maybe he's not angry. Maybe he just feels passionately about the volunteer program.

"Remember, you are the first line of contact. You volunteers are going to be the face of this city. Now go out there and make this city proud. But first, go get your free meal."

We all applaud.

After dinner, a mood of dizzy confusion hangs over the volunteers jammed in the disorganized line in the softly lit, plush-carpeted hallway.

"So when you went to sign up for this," Cerise asks, "did you have to pay the $25 fee too?"

"Yep. It's like paying to work for free." I dangle my purse from my finger and watch swing it back and forth. "But who knows what cool stuff could happen?" I feel a tingle of excitement growing in me.

"That's right!" Cerise grins. "Anything is possible. You just gotta believe. I'm gonna sign up to be an usher."

I flip through the leaflet of assignment possibilities. Hmmm, VIP driver has a nice ring to it. The line gets shorter until finally I can step up to the volunteer assignment table.

"Hi there. I'd like to sign up for a VIP driver shift."

"Sure. Oh, and here!" The woman behind the table hands me a green plastic water bottle. "It's your swag."

Swag? Visions of free CDs, band T-shirts and chocolate burst in my head.

"Looks like we only have one VIP driver slot left."

"I'll take it! When does it start?"

"6:30 a.m.," the lady says.

Chapter Three

NEVER MIND THE fact that I'm *so* not an extrovert. And forget that I'm terrible at making small talk with random strangers. Nope, none of that matters because today I'm going to be a new me. Bold! Courageous!

And what's even more awesome is the Jegg organizers told me I get some sort of swanky car to drive, and hey, as for the 6:30 to 11 a.m. shift, well, I'm a morning person anyway.

Before I get into my Focus to head downtown, I dab on some Wonderstruck perfume for luck, then ask the universe to allow me to cross paths with Michael Bublé and Taylor Swift. Who knows what could happen? I feel that old familiar tingle of possibilities seduce me.

I drive downtown and the buzz of anticipation hums through me as I make my way over to command central—the lobby of the Delta Hotel.

I bound into the room, smiling at everyone I see. This is so exciting.

The girl in charge (nametag: Renee), hands me my two-way radio. As I feel its weight in my hand, the first doubt of the day surfaces. Uh, how do you use these things?

I fiddle with the dial, finally clicking it onto the right channel. Task accomplished, I search for someplace to put the heavy device. Who forgot to wear pants with belt loops? Yep, that'd be me. My enthusiasm takes another dip. But never mind. I'm sure once I get out there in my swanky car, it'll all be great. Right?

Wrong.

It's huge. And it's not a car. Swallowing, I clamber in to the giant SUV, noting with a twinge of fear that it's twice as long and twice as tall as my Focus. And now I feel twice as intimidated about all of this. But it's too late. This is, literally, what I signed up for.

Taking a deep breath, I insert the key into the ignition and head to the gas station as instructed. I rumble the tank—er, I mean, SUV—up to each intersection, feeling like I could just barrel through them. No, no. I need to use the brake. Damn these false-confidence building vehicles. You get hit by a semi, you're still toast. Doesn't matter the size of the grill.

But driving in a straight line isn't so bad. God forbid I might have to change lanes, though. The magnetic signs with VIP Courtesy Shuttle written on them are blocking my shoulder check abilities. I'll have to rely solely on my mirrors. Isn't that something they tell you not to do in driver's ed? Well, I can't do anything about that now.

Back from the gas station, Renee gives me my first pickup, Jill. She's going to the exhibition grounds from the Wyngate Hotel. Easy enough.

I head back out to the giant SUV. Get in and take all of thirty seconds going the block from the Delta to the Wyngate.

I go in to the front desk. "I'm here to pick up Jill.

I'm with the Jegg VIP courtesy shuttle service."

The front desk girl gives me a blank look.

Um, what? I thought they were supposed to know what was going on. But before I embarrass myself further, I hear the click of heels on tile.

"Jill?"

She nods.

Whew. That was lucky. We head outside again. Just in time, I remember I'm supposed to be all white-glove, so I rush to open her door for her and let her get settled. Scurrying back around to the driver's seat, I say a silent prayer of protection as I merge the big beast into traffic.

My tension soon eases as Jill and I make light small talk.

Until…

I get to the intersection of Albert Street and Saskatchewan Drive. My brain freezes. Oh no. Are the exhibition grounds here, or is it one street up? Crap. Why can't I remember? Now, of all times, to forget. Argh.

The hamster in my brain is running faster and faster, going nowhere but in circles as I push for the answer. Thankfully, it's a red light so I can think. Or draw a blank, actually.

When the light turns green, I suddenly remember. Thank God. It *is* this street. To the left and up the hill. Breathe. Just breathe. I check the rearview. Jill is oblivious. Good.

After dropping her off, I'm idling at an intersection when a city bus drives by with a giant ad on its side. And I gasp. Right there in front of me, larger than life, is Taylor Swift.

Further up the street, a billboard captures my attention. Yep, that's right. In his suit, holding a Jegg award, is Michael Bublé.

I laugh aloud in the silence. I totally just got to see *both* Taylor Swift and Michael Bublé. Nice sense of humor, universe. Nice.

Still smiling, I manage to parallel park (about three feet too far from the curb) in the shuttle queue and go back inside. I'm in for a bit of a wait, I discover. Apparently none of the glitterati want to go much of anywhere at 9 a.m. on a Friday morning.

One of the other drivers at my table starts chatting with me about music and concerts. "My wife and I are big country fans."

"Oh yeah? I'm a big Taylor Swift fan."

"We got to meet her."

I lean forward. "No way. Really? How did it happen?"

He shrugs. "My wife is a fan of hers more than me. We were on the escalator in the mall and my wife nudges me and says, 'Isn't that...?' Sure enough, we look over and it's Taylor. So it was a 'hi, how are you' sort of thing."

"Wow, that's so cool." Once again, the universe has been listening. This guy's actually *met* Taylor Swift. I'm getting closer to my dream. This is definitely another sign.

"Vicky?"

I jump up as Renee motions me over. "We need you to go over to this address—" she hands me a piece of paper with an address scribbled on it "—and pick up Farley and McCloud, party of 2, at 11 a.m."

My shift ends at 11 a.m. Should I tell her that? I

ignore the vague sense of discomfort in my stomach, because I really want to do this. I can't miss out on even one moment of excitement. So I just say, "Got it."

After some pacing and staring into space, 10:40 rolls around. Whatever. I'm going over there now. Give myself plenty of time, just in case. I don't want to be late, after all.

I get to the hotel ten minutes later. Riiiight. That was too much time.

My stomach clenches as I get out and head into the hotel lobby. What do I even say to these random strangers? And how will I identify Farley and McCloud, party of two?

The clock above the desk says it's now 11 a.m. Except no one's come down. I begin pacing. Soon it's five after.

Where are they? Have I missed them? Do I need to like, go and tell someone? Deciding to do neither, I keep pacing. Five more minutes pass. Ack. This is torture.

A guy in his late twenties approaches me. Here we go. He seems to take up much more room than his five-foot-nine frame would call for. His artfully disarrayed blond strands almost perfectly match his caramel-colored leather jacket that looks suspiciously like a replica of Mick Jagger's.

Why did I sign up for this again? I swallow.

"I'm Farley," he says, looking me up and down as if I should be screaming his name in some mosh pit somewhere, my lighter—er, smartphone—held aloft.

I just nod, fumbling with the car remote.

I hit the unlock button a second too late and wince

when he tugs on the handle and it doesn't open, He shoots me an annoyed look. God, he's going to think I'm completely lame. I hastily cover my *faux pas* with a professional mask that falls into place as I slide into the driver's seat. If I pretend to know what I'm doing, he'll be convinced, too.

I rattle my seatbelt into place with slippery palms, hiding a smile. I'm more nervous about the damn SUV maneuverability than this supposed rock star beside me. Who is he, anyway? Certainly he has all of the bravado, but none of the class of an elite entertainer.

Could he really be up for a Jegg? Well, I guess they're not based on personality. If that were the case, Eric Black would've won for being a hottie and a sweetheart. Every year. In every category. But I'm not on the nominations committee. And I digress.

I frown to myself—my estimation of Farley might be a tad unfair. After all, I don't know him. I park outside the entrance while we wait for McCloud.

"And what's your name?" Farley's tone has all the subtleness of a man sure of his charms and his quarry. But clueless quarry I'm not.

"Vicky."

He doesn't shake my hand; instead he opts to lean in too close to me. I nearly gag on his heavy cologne.

"You know," his voice lowers in what he probably thinks is a seductive tone, "some people call me Zed. But I'll let you in on a little secret—that's my stage name. My real first name, well, that remains a secret."

I shift away from him, ignoring the slight tremble in my hands from his invasion of my personal space, while denying him the pleasure of a surprised-but-pleased fangirl smile at his false invitation of intimacy.

The sound of the back door opening has Farley sliding back to his side of the vehicle.

I exhale in relief. This must be McCloud. Certainly his eyes are a cloudless blue, I notice, as our gazes meet. No, wait. His eyes are actually green...

"Hey," he says with an easy grin. And suddenly, I want to throw open my door, climb into the backseat and hug him.

Of course, I don't.

"Hi," I return, ripping my eyes away from his and back to the road.

I put the SUV into drive and ease out of the parking lot.

"Here's the plan." Farley starts talking before McCloud can say anything. "We need to go to Shopper's Drug Mart and then pick up some guitars and then go to Campbell High School."

I'm only supposed to drop them off, not chauffer them to three different places. Besides, I don't have time. I have to be at the temp agency for an interview at 12:30 and it's already 11:20. Uh-oh. Time to lay down the rules. "I can drop you at Shopper's and then you can call and get someone else to pick you up from there."

"Oh, Shopper's will just be five minutes," Farley assures me. "We need to pick up our meds. McCloud has an insane toothache and my sciatic nerve is killing me." Farley's eyes widen in a pleading look.

"Ouch," I murmur. In a normal voice, I say, "Sure. Five minutes, no problem."

"It's Andrea, right?" Farley is leaning across the console again. He seems to have forgotten I'm driving, not out for drinks.

"Nope. Vicky."

"Right. I knew that." Farley flashes a perfect pearly white smile.

McCloud clears his throat. We've arrived at the drug store.

"Go on in, McCloud." Farley doesn't spare him a backward glance. "Vicky and I are just going to wait here."

McCloud's door slams. The sun beats through the windshield. As in all cases of social situational terror, I begin babbling about the weather. Farley rolls down the window. "It's hot in here. Go get me a water. Needs to be Evian."

I did volunteer for this, after all. So I head to the grocery section of Shopper's. No Evian. Oh crap.

I head back to the SUV. "They didn't have Evian."

"So you didn't get me anything?" He frowns.

"But you said—"

He holds up a hand and I stop speaking. Fine. Be like that. I cross my arms. Silent minutes pass. Or is it hours? I can't tell the difference anymore. That's what too little sleep and too many nerves'll do to a girl. I roll down my window too. Remember too late I was supposed to radio back to command central that I've got my people. Oops.

Before I can pick up the radio, a flurry of motion catches my periphery. It's a homeless man at Farley's rolled-down window. "Got five bucks?" He puts his hand out toward Farley. Farley jolts back in surprise and shakes his head.

"Jesus! Homeless people," Farley mutters as the man walks away.

Quiet descends again.

In the rearview mirror I see McCloud coming back to the vehicle. I can't help but stare at him as he walks across the parking lot. What is wrong with me? He should look sloppy with his windblown black hair, ripped jeans and untucked soft gray T-shirt. But somehow, it just enhances his hotness. He opens the rear passenger door.

But now Farley hops out.

McCloud gets into the back seat and holds up a pill bottle. "Do you know how many hours apart I'm supposed to take these pills? It says three times a day."

He expects me to know that? I have no clue. But his cluelessness is kind of cute. As I turn to face him, I catch a whiff of fresh laundry and Ivory soap. His scent. Mmmm...

"Um, at each meal? Or something?" I meet his gaze and wish I could just dive right into those sea-green depths. Calm relaxation seeps through my body.

McCloud's about to reply but the moment shatters because Farley gets back in, Perrier in hand. "You could've gotten me this," he mutters low enough that McCloud can't hear, and uncaps the bottle.

I force myself to ignore that and stay in professional mode. "All set?" I don't wait for a response to my rhetorical question.

"That sun is nice and warm. The great weather must be thanks to our fabulous driver," McCloud says from the back seat.

The unexpected praise has a laugh bubbling out of me. "Thanks!"

"Do you know where the Artful Dodger is?" Farley asks.

Somehow, I don't think he's talking about Dickens' *Great Expectations* character.

Crap. Informed driver, I am not. I've never even heard of that place. Luckily, the volunteer committee thought of that. I bless them as I scramble for my clipboard with its music venue addresses tucked under the steel hinge. Stomping on the brake a little too hard as we hit a red light, I pry the brochure loose with the fingers of one hand while keeping an eye on the intersection with the other.

"You don't even know where it is? Don't you even live in this city?" Farley frowns.

"Yes, I do live here. I've just never been *there*." I smile through gritted teeth.

"I'm sure she'll be able to figure it out in a minute, man. Just give her a sec."

I flash a grateful smile in McCloud's direction and then frown at the brochure. 2863 11th Avenue? Umm. Is 11th north or south of 13th Avenue? I glance at the console, but I have no idea how to use the GPS that's built into it. Crap. Crap. Crap. *Think, think, think, brain.* Now is not the time to space out on me. Especially not in the middle of traffic.

Pressing my sweaty fingers to the radio talk button, I ask directions in a whisper that I wish McCloud and Farley couldn't hear. Am I a tourist instead of a native? You'd think it.

I pull up to the right place at last.

"We'll only be a minute," Farley calls over his shoulder when he gets out, closely followed by McCloud.

Yeah. That's what you said the last time. I turn off the engine.

I drum my fingers on the steering wheel. So this is how the other half lives. Or at least, the rock star stratosphere. You know, maybe I'm judging Farley too harshly. Maybe the life of a rock star requires one to be all attitude and no altruism. But is it a persona...or is it fear and insecurity masquerading as swagger? And why is McCloud putting up with it?

I take a deep breath, glad for the empty car and the quiet, and try to regain the modicum of composure I'd somehow lost getting up at 5 a.m. It's now 12:01, way past my official end of shift. Command central is not going to be happy. But the VIPs are. And to be honest, so am I. It *is* kind of fun. When I'm not getting lost or fending off come-ons.

I see McCloud approaching and my heart does an extra beat. He opens the front passenger door. Two extra beats. I don't say a word. My expression must be saying something, though, because he looks straight at me. "I'm riding shotgun now."

A little tingle zips down my spine.

Farley joins us a few moments later. "So the guitars we were supposed to pick up here are actually over at the Delta Hotel." He flips back his shaggy bangs, making his hair even more artfully disarrayed—if that's possible.

"That gonna work for you?" McCloud checks my face.

12:05. Who cares if I'm late to that interview? I'd agree to anything now that he's beside me, now that the delicious relaxed warmth is flowing through me again, now that he's close enough to touch. But my palms brush the steering wheel instead of his skin.

I steer into traffic again and a few moments pass

in ringing silence. Damn. Do they want the radio on? There are more dials on the giant SUV's instrument panel than a 747 and I don't dare touch anything. I might break it. Or trip some sort of weird alarm.

McCloud breaks the silence. "So what do you do when you're not driving around crazy musicians?"

As I watch his calm confidence and sincere curiosity, he not only understands that craziness but he's accepted it. And his place in it—right in the middle of the music world. I give him a smile—a genuine one that I've been saving up. "Right now I'm getting ready to do some temping. But I'm really a writer."

"A writer? Awesome. What are you working on? I'm writing a play. It's a lot harder than writing a song, that's for sure. There's so much detail there to capture. You can really go in-depth."

"Yeah, you really can." For some reason, I feel like I can tell him anything. "I'm working on a novel. Very cool that you're writing a play. What's it about?"

McCloud launches into enthusiastic detail. "It has to do with early rock and roll musicians in the 1950s and the Cold War. It's gonna be a musical."

"That's great! Sounds like a nice artistic challenge."

"Yep. So—"

"Oh, I tried writing a novel once," Farley cuts in from the backseat. "But my publisher said the thing about writing a novel is, well, you have to write it first."

"Yes," I agree politely, willing myself not to frown when I look at him in the rearview mirror.

But what's this? A tiny flicker of pain skitters across his expression as he slumps back in his seat. A ping of compassion nudges my heart. Maybe he's simply afraid of not being noticed. Or of no longer being the center of attention. Perhaps he feels threatened by the mutual appreciation society being formed in the front seat. Maybe he thinks it's a barrier he isn't allowed across, a divide he can't conquer, no matter how much swagger and superstar attitude he fronts to the world.

Maybe he isn't a jerk. Maybe he's just afraid no one will love him.

McCloud continues as if uninterrupted. "So what's your novel about?"

"It's set in 1940s Chicago." I blush. "It was inspired by an Eric Black jazz song." I don't dare say that I want to give Eric a copy of the story—as a sort of thank-you for helping me get over my writer's block.

"That's very cool."

"Wow. Awesome." This from Farley. No doubt trying to top McCloud's statement.

We're at the Delta. And I realize too late—we're trapped. I stare at the bevy of service vehicles blocking the only exit. Why did I not see that when I drove in? "Oops," I mutter. "Now how do I get out of here?"

McCloud says quietly, "Why don't we go get the guitars and then you can figure out what you need to do to get out of this spot?"

Grateful for his perceptive suggestion, I nod, and they set off.

After repositioning the SUV, I jump when, a few minutes later, the passenger door opens and Farley leans in. "We're getting coffees. What do you drink?"

An image of that bald volunteer coordinator pounding the podium flashes through my mind. Do not accept gratuities or gifts. Ever.

Does this count? But I want a drink. "Um, uh, well, er..." I make a fumble for my purse. If I pay, it'll be all right.

Farley sees the movement and frowns. "No, no. Come on."

Just make a decision already, Vicky. "Um...blue—berry tea?"

"Blueberry tea. Got it."

"Thank you!" Now who's sounding like a fangirl? Argh. And I still don't bloody know who he is. All earlier compassion for him evaporates. Damn him and his attitude, making me feel like I should know every last detail of his life, like I should bow to his godliness for spending $3.99 on me. Okay, so maybe that's just my own prejudice talking, thanks to the scars Jason gave me. Even so, Farley's cockiness still pisses me off.

Before I can pull out my phone to Google him so I can at least know who the hell he thinks he is, a group of shaggy-haired guys who look like they belong in 1975 walk by. Their heads are down, their beards tugged by the breeze. It's The Sheepdogs. The only reason I recognize them, though, is from that music magazine cover I'd seen at the bookstore the other day.

The back hatch rattles and I see McCloud and Farley loading up the elusive guitars.

They get back in, giving me my tea and sipping their coffees. McCloud, I notice, goes for the front seat again. I grin. Farley just lost out on that little

contest.

"So..." McCloud says, studying me for a moment. His eyes are even greener at this distance. And who knew an eyebrow piercing could be so...appealing? I've never been into men with metal before.

So...*what's your number*? Or—my mind leaps to the next hope—*do you want to go to dinner*? I hold my breath, willing his next words to be that.

"So what else are you working on? Have you had anything published?"

Sigh. "Well, I wrote a few songs—okay, actually just the lyrics—and some poems," I find myself easily admitting to him. "Haven't had any fiction published yet, but I'm getting close to completing my book's first draft. So I decided it's time to start sending out query letters to publishers. Oh! And I want to try to get an agent."

"Oh yeah?"

I nod, feeling the admiration in his gaze.

"So wow, you've written a novel. That's great. I tried writing a novel once. It turned out to be three pages."

We both laugh.

"You know, I have a great deal of respect for writers." He looks over at me again.

I blush at his compliment. And grin again. "Thanks."

Whoops. Did he mean me or just writers in general? Argh. Will he think I have a huge ego now?

Fortunately, he continues talking. "Songs are all surface—you can't go into detail. But with prose, it's all *about* detail. You can describe a flower for three pages. Songwriting isn't like that."

I nod. "I'm a big fan of Taylor Swift because she does all her own songwriting. I'd love to actually write songs like hers."

Farley cuts in. "You know how they wrote 'Fifteen'? How she got all those girls to fall in love with her? It wasn't just her, she doesn't write her own songs."

He bursts my bubble from the backseat. What? How can that be? Damn him. Yet another reason to dislike him.

Perhaps McCloud senses my shock and disappointment because he clarifies. "She doesn't write *all* her own songs. She writes some of them. The songwriters she worked with took pieces of things. They read her diary. I know. I've been in the room."

The same room as... Wait, that means... Oh. My. God. McCloud, this guy sitting next to me... Me! Has been in the same room as *Taylor Swift* when she's writing songs? Oh. My. God. I forget to watch the road, forget I'm even in a car, let alone driving it as I sort of just stare at him. Wordless.

Thank God this tub practically steers itself. Otherwise we probably would've swerved into oncoming traffic by now. I swallow and manage a demure, "Oh yeah? That's cool," before remembering to signal and turn the corner on my way to their third, and what I believe is their final, destination, Campbell High School.

Farley says, "Actually, our show's not till 1:30, so is there a coffee shop near here? We can just wait there."

The mantra of "just smile and nod and do what they say" is so embedded into my psyche from the training session that Farley's changing his mind once again doesn't even register. So I blithely say, "Oh yeah, there's one just around the corner."

"No, wait." Farley speaks again. "It would be redundant to go into a coffee shop holding coffees. We have plenty of time. Let's go to a music store."

A music store. Well, that's easy. There's HMV in the mall, which is just downtown a few blocks.

"Yeah," McCloud agrees. "Do you know if there's a Long & McQuade in town?"

Who? What? Where? My mind revs into overdrive once more, trying to think fast and talk faster, all the while struggling to appear calm and professional. Multitasking under pressure is *so* not my gig.

I pick up the radio again. "Car 11. So, we've had a change of plans. We're looking for a music store now. Long & McQuade. There one here?"

"Roger that, Car 11. On McIntyre and 8th."

Huh? I can't exactly look at Googlemaps on my phone and drive at the same time, so I ask instead. "McIntyre and 8th? Where is that, exactly?"

"It's off of Dewdney Avenue."

That means absolutely nothing to me. Meanwhile, while I'm trying to shake the fuzz out of my mental GPS, I'm hitting every green light in a six-block radius. So I just keep driving through them. Losing track of where I really am as my mind desperately churns for a street location it has no idea the whereabouts of.

The mic crackles to life again. "Car 11, once you get to the music store, we're sending another driver to pick up your party. Your shift's long over."

"We don't want another driver," both McCloud and Farley chorus, practically drowning out the dispatcher. Never mind the fact that she can't hear them.

Where the hell is this Long & McQuade? Driving aimlessly hasn't given me any insight. I radio in again. "Um, could you specify the exact location? I'm not too clear."

"Where are you now, Car 11?"

"I'm headed west on Victoria. I'll be approaching the intersection with Elphinstone in a few blocks."

"We need a landmark. Where's the nearest landmark?"

"Um, well, I don't know. Like I said, I'll be coming up on Elphinstone soon."

"Car 11, just pull over. We're sending someone else to take your party to Long & McQuade. He's on his way now."

That's it then. I'm a complete failure. Why did I ever agree to be a driver anyway? So much for glamorous. More like hopeless. Damn it. I guess I asked one too many questions.

I signal and pull over. Talk about an awkward silence. Crap. Well, they'll certainly remember their Jegg experience now. What am I supposed to say here? Sorry, but I don't actually know this city at all? Sorry, but I hope you get to your gig on time because I've wasted an extra twenty minutes with aimless driving? I sigh inwardly. But hey, on the bright side, at least I haven't started crying.

A blaring car horn shatters the silence. I jerk my head around. Gak! I'm actually still in the turning lane. My shot nerves didn't process that fact until like, now.

"You might want to park at that Dairy Queen." McCloud nods to the restaurant across the street, his tone matter-of-fact, yet reassuring.

I steer the behemoth into a spot, hoping I haven't crushed any small children licking ice cream cones. 'Cuz you wouldn't feel it in this thing.

In my bravest, most professional voice, I say, "If I would've known where the music store was, I could've taken you guys there. I apologize."

McCloud turns to me. "It's okay. We're fine. We have plenty of time till our gig." He pauses. "This isn't your car, is it?"

I shake my head, relief whooshing through me. He understands. Now I really want to hug him. I give a nervous laugh. "I drive a Ford Focus."

Before anyone can say anything else, I see another VIP shuttle behind us.

They get out and I can't help but feel a twinge of sadness. Wishing McCloud and I had met under different circumstances. And in a different vehicle. One that I'm not driving.

He turns back to me, and to my surprise, extends his hand. "Good luck with your novel." His green eyes rest on mine.

"Thank you." I smile at him. "Have a good time this weekend. And good luck."

Not to be beaten, Farley whirls around and sticks out his hand too. "Good luck with everything."

"You too," I say. "Have a good weekend."

The doors slam. As I watch them both walk away, I know exactly who the real rock star is.

✧ ✧ ✧

IT'S ONLY LATER, after vacuuming out the car's interior, that I discover a crumpled business card on the floor.

I pick it up:

McCloud Xavier
Producer/ Songwriter/Multi-instrumentalist
ThunderCloud Music, 4656 89th Street West
Toronto, ON M6X 2D8 904-587-8904
mccloud@thundercloudmusic.com

I can't help myself—I tuck it into my purse.
Later that day I give in to my curiosity and find, through my shameless Googling, a Wikipedia entry.

McCloud Xavier, one of the Canadian music industry's rising songwriting talents, started out playing music at age 8, began writing songs at 12, formed his first band at 15, and then at the age of 21 signed his first multi-million dollar songwriting deal. Xavier, who is now 28, owns his own record label, ThunderCloud Music, and works with various artists including up-and-coming Canadian rocker Zed Farley. He has shared both the studio and the stage with Barenaked Ladies, Great Big Sea and Maroon 5. He also had the privilege of collaborating with Paul Anka. McCloud has won five Jeggs and had a Grammy nomination. He wrote two top-ten singles and one number-one hit, and has had three songs appear in Hollywood feature films.

Who knows? Maybe I'll run into McCloud again. when I become best friends with Taylor Swift? Hey, the universe works in mysterious ways.

Chapter Four

IT'S FINALLY MAY—AMAZING how slowly six months can go by when you're waiting for someone—er, some*thing* really awesome. I don't have to wait any longer, though, because the big day has arrived at last.

I grin at my reflection in the mirror as I rustle through my makeup bag, applying foundation, powder and lipstick. (In a nice kissable pink shade.) Eeee! This is so fun! The butterflies in my stomach flutter their agreement.

See, this is how I'm *supposed* to feel getting ready for a date. (Er, concert.)

I pause, considering. Should I wear my contacts instead of my glasses? I don't want to seem like I'm trying too hard or anything.

Because I mean, you know, I don't want to feel stupid afterward. And I definitely don't want to be wearing my contacts just to try to impress Eric Black.

Oh hell. Who am I kidding?

Of *course* I'm going to wear my contacts. And of *course* I'm doing it to impress him. I have to look my best.

Driven by that internal craving for deep, soul-defining love, I pop in my contacts and blot my lipstick.

I check the clock on the nightstand. 7:20. Argh! How did time get away from me so quickly?

I run the brush through my brunette curls one final time, making sure my part's exactly straight, and then head out the door with Cerise.

✧ ✧ ✧

I DO A little twirl in my retro dress, savoring the feel of the cherry-print fabric swirling around my legs as I wait beside Cerise in the lobby of the casino lounge, my Eric Black ticket in hand.

"Oh, this VIP thing is going to rock." I pat my purse, a copy of the *Lyrics of Love* 109-page manuscript tucked safely inside, all ready to give to Eric.

I can't help giggling to myself. All the articles I've read and videos I've compulsively—okay, maybe a little obsessively—watched of Eric Black, tell me that not only is he an awesome singer, but also that he seems to be unattached—oh, and we have so many common interests: writing, culture, jazz, travel. (And, oh my God, he likes to cook. What is sexier than a man in the kitchen? Mmm, well, maybe a *half-naked* man in the kitchen...but I digress.)

What's even better is he knows what it's like to be a writer. After all, he said in one of his interviews, "I'm happiest when I'm alone and writing." Me too. And he said he wants to have a family. And he seems so humble, too. Therefore, we're like, perfect for each other... We could even be soul mates.

I shake my head. Wait. I haven't even met him yet. Can't go overboard here. I'm twenty-four, not fourteen.

✧ ✧ ✧

I RESIST THE urge to wipe my sweaty hands on the pristine white damask tablecloth draped over the round VIP table Cerise and I are seated at, in a room backstage at the casino.

I swallow and check my lipstick for the umpteenth time.

Breathe, Vicky, just breathe.

Cerise is busy chatting with our tablemate, some woman named Sylvia. How can Cerise stay so calm? (Probably because she's not obsessed with Eric like I am. And because she's an extrovert.)

Suddenly, the door opens.

Oh God—he's right there! And he's wearing...runners? A black track jacket zipped halfway? Over top of a green V-neck T-shirt and a pair of jeans? *Sigh*. I guess he can't exactly wear a tux 24/7.

"Hey, guys! Thanks for coming out. It means a lot to me that you've all chosen to support tonight's cause—the Canadian Heart and Stroke Foundation."

There's a small smattering of applause. Canadians. Always awesome at being all polite and respectful.

"Got some surprise guests for you guys tonight." He gestures to the door and four other musicians walk in.

Sara Schlessenger. Rob Martin. Darren Ward. And...

I blink and frown. *He* can't be here.

No.

I shake my head.

But the man with the artfully disarrayed blond hair walks into the room. Why is Zed Farley here supporting the Heart and Stroke Foundation? I didn't think he had a heart. Okay, that was a bit harsh...

I join in with the second round of applause as they all file into the room. Eric joins in with applause too, as he says, "I also want to say thanks to my friends in the music industry who've chosen to support me, and this cause, by being a part of it too."

Then all five musicians begin moving among the tables, talking to people. Shaking hands. Laughing. Smiling. But my eyes are glued to Eric.

Cerise leans toward me and whispers. "He's smokin'."

I grin. I knew she'd think so.

My grin turns to a frown when I see who she's eyeing.

"Cerise," I whisper. "Farley's a real jerk. Believe me."

Cerise just smiles. "Oh, those are the most *fun*."

I shake my head and give her a playful nudge. She's always been attracted to bad boys. I turn my attention back to Eric. He's laughing and joking with people two tables over. When will he come over here so I can give him *Lyrics of Love*?

"So what do you do?" It's the lady who's sitting next to me at our table. Sylvia.

"I'm temping at a few different offices in town while I work on my fiction. I'm a writer."

"Good for you. What do you write?"

I study my fingernails. "Romance?" I clear my throat. "I mean, romance. What about you?"

"My husband and I run a llama farm. And I'm an acquisitions editor. I also happen to love jazz. But that's obvious, considering I'm here."

"An acquisitions editor? That's like, the craziest coincidence, meeting here like this."

She shrugs. "Eh. I don't believe in that stuff. Anyway, it's just a small e-publisher based in Toronto."

"But you're from Saskatchewan, right?"

"Gotta love telecommuting." She pulls out a business card. "We're pretty small, so we publish lots of genres. And we're always looking for new authors. Send me some of your work." She slides the card across the table. "We like unique stuff, and I can guarantee I'll give you my honest opinion. No fluff here." She laughs.

I take her card and tuck it into my purse. "Thanks."

Hmmm. Should I give her my manuscript right now? No. I want Eric to be the first to see it.

I'm only half paying attention to my own thoughts, because now Eric's moving in this direction.

Closer.

Closer.

I crane my neck.

And—

He walks right by our table. *Argh*. This is supposed to be a VIP meet and greet, not a game of musical chairs. Is he avoiding our table? Considering the unreasonable amount of time I've been covertly staring at him—he probably *is* avoiding it.

All of a sudden, the scent of an expensive cologne drifts past and over me. Woodsy. Spicy. Warm. Rich. My skin prickles and I inhale. My eyes drift closed. And though I've never smelled it before in my life, I know exactly what it's called. *Eucris...*

❖   ❖   ❖

THE SMOOTH FROSTED glass bottle rests heavy in my gloved palm, the department store lights glow softly, spreading a calm over the bustle of shoppers.

"Eucris. It's the very best, miss. Imported from Paris," the salesgirl assures me. "Perfect for your fella."

I hand her a crisp five-dollar bill. "I'll take it."

◇　◇　◇

A NUDGE STARTLES the vision away. "Vicky." It's Cerise. "Don't fall asleep yet. The show's not even started."

"Huh? I wasn't asleep." I look around guiltily. Was I?

Cerise doesn't hear me, because she's now shamelessly flirting with Farley. I hear her throaty laugh as he gives her a glass of wine from the nearby refreshment table.

Don't encourage him, Cerise. But it's too late; he's already scribbling down her number on a napkin. He winks at her as he walks away.

I stifle a groan.

Eucris. I frown. I'm getting to the bottom of this. I dig out my iPhone and bring up Google.

Something bumping into the back of my chair jars me, and the iPhone clatters to the floor.

"Oops. Sorry about that." Eric leans over and picks up my phone. "These things are expensive. Nope, not broken." He grins and hands it back to me. But then he turns away.

"So what grade are you in?"

Huh?

I dart my eyes to the left. *Oh.*

How cute. Eric's talking to a little girl at the table directly behind me. She's happily chattering about the artwork she'd just completed at school that day, her blonde ponytail bobbing with eagerness.

They're adorable together. I swallow a lump in my throat. He straightens up from his crouched position by her chair and scrawls his autograph for her.

As he hands it to her, her eyes light up and she giggles. "Thank you." She ducks her head.

"You're welcome." He smiles.

Tears prickle in my eyes. I surreptitiously wipe them away, then whip out my compact and pray my mascara hasn't smudged. Nope. All good.

I toss the compact back into my purse next to my rolled-up manuscript and raise my eyes only to discover Eric's at our table at last.

"Hi, there." He places his hands palm-down against the tabletop and leans toward the three of us, smiling. He's not wearing a ring.

I shut my mouth and swallow, my throat suddenly gone dry. Mostly due to the fact that from this vantage point, I can totally see the bit of chest hair that's just visible at the point of his V-neck T-shirt.

"And how are you guys?"

He swivels his head in my and Cerise's direction and heat floods my cheeks. Almost involuntarily, I lick my lips, straighten my spine and lift my chest.

His brown eyes meet mine, and I watch as his gaze moves for the tiniest nanosecond from my eyes down to my chest and back up again to my face. *Score! Eric Black just checked me out.* Yet it's in the precise moment that he meets my gaze again that there's a flicker of...something...in his eyes. Recognition?

Confusion? Admiration?

I manage to croak out, "I'm good." But before I can add anything else, or really understand what, exactly, I saw in his gaze, he's already straightened back up and is looking at the clock. "Well, I'd better go and get ready."

He walks over to the refreshment table and grabs a couple of slices of marbled cheese. "Gotta have some cheese with my pre-show wine." He pops a slice in his mouth.

No. This can't be the end.

What am I going to do now? Do I just shove my manuscript under his nose and be like, "Here! I wrote this! Read it!"? I want him to give it the attention it deserves. I want him to *appreciate* it. I don't want him to just barely cast a glance at it and then throw it away because he has to go onstage in five minutes.

But it's too late to do anything. He's walking out the door and we're all following along behind him.

He gestures toward the hallway that leads back to the foyer. "Well, enjoy the show, guys!"

I force myself to walk down the hallway. *Crap. Crap. Crap.* Now my opportunity is completely gone and—

No, Vicky. No. Don't do this. I know perfectly well that there are no guarantees and I need to just let it go—just let all my expectations go and enjoy the show. Because that's what I really came for. Right?

❖ ❖ ❖

CERISE AND I make our way down the aisle to the very front cluster of tables and find seats 11 and 12. I settle in, relieved that the view is perfect, not too far and not too close to the stage.

And what a stage.

The black velvet curtains are drawn back to reveal the bright white stage lights that glint off the candy-apple red drum set and the gold cymbals that hang suspended above the drums, while the bass violin—or is it a cello? I always get them confused—lays on its side, its satiny smooth wooden curves gently kissed by the soft orange backlights.

And the pièce de résistance—the piano.

A full-size Yamaha grand. It's a beaut. As the lights twinkle down on it from above, creating contrasting shadows and sparkles on its curves, it simply sits, just waiting for a certain man with a magic touch to awaken the hidden longings from the deep core of its soul. A sigh escapes me.

"Excuse me?"

I jump and look up to see an older lady with short black hair standing nearby. Gak! Interrupted in the middle of my fantasy again. Maybe the universe is trying to tell me something?

She addresses me. "Is this seat 13?"

"Oh, yes." I smile at her. She sits down in the empty seat.

And then I forget everything else as Eric comes out, wearing a perfectly tailored gray pinstripe suit with a blue tie. His brown wavy hair contrasts so nicely with the crisp whiteness of his shirt. (God, there is nothing hotter than a man who wears a suit well.)

He picks up the microphone and looks out into the crowd. "How are you doing?" My heart lurches.

"I'm awesome," some lady shouts from five rows back, "now that you're here!" My sentiments exactly.

"We've got a great show for you tonight." He grins, then sits down at the piano and puts those long fingers on the ivories.

Oh my God. All I can do is stare. The notes just seem to spill out of him—through his lips, through his fingers—as if by some sort of alchemy; like he's the master who releases the floodgates, the man who unlocks the doorway into another world. Another world that's filled to overflowing with music. Glorious music.

My eyes start to prickle with unshed tears. Such sweet notes. One after the other, running and chasing and blurring together as they leap from the instrument and directly into my heart. I hear gasps all around me—or are they my own?—as the melody increases pace. The drums and the cello keep up easily and effortlessly as the tempo slides upward yet again. And now again. And *again*.

Faster and faster and faster until my head is spinning, my heart is pounding and beads of sweat are forming all over my body; my fingers are trembling and my feet are tapping, tapping, tapping as if they can somehow leap up of their own accord and begin dancing, dancing, dancing. Just that rhythm. Oh that dear, gorgeous rhythm. That melody. Oh God.

My breathing speeds and my chest heaves as I continue to watch him, transfixed. Completely and utterly. He goes faster and faster still, until I don't see how his fingers can move that quickly, until it becomes not a man and an instrument, but a fluid melding of Divine and human.

I feel my heart swelling, swelling, swelling until I know it's going to burst out of my chest for the sheer joy of it all. Ah, ah, ah, this music. This *music*. The drummer and the bassist fill in around those piano notes, speeding away, speeding, speeding, speeding—

And then suddenly silence. Nothing. Not even a pin drop.

Chapter Five

FALL BACK in my chair, a tear rolling down my cheek.

And my heart, oh yes, my heart has just shattered on the floor, the quivering pieces are lying there just waiting to be reassembled by the new notes falling ever so slowly, one by one, into my senses.

My brain struggles to grasp the momentum of the moment as the barest touch of his fingers on the keyboard evokes a trail of sensation within me; the merest whisper of his voice sends a soaring crescendo flying up from me and outward like waves ripping on an endless pond.

Impossibly, I feel my heart break again, each tiny shard emitting a pulsing light of its own as it, too, begins vibrating and surrendering to the frenetic, frenzied pace that's begun, yet again.

I watch the sweat dripping down the side of his face even as I feel a trickle of my own perspiration run down my spine.

Ugh. I'm sweating. And so is he. But my body sends shiver of delight, not revulsion, coursing through me.

He towels the sweat away in the pause between numbers. And then it gets even better. Because now he's singing his latest song—my favorite.

I sing the words along with him, watching his lips,

so close to the microphone, wishing that microphone was me, wishing he was the one kissing my lips, pressing against me...

The song ends. "We're going to take a break."

A collective groan comes from the audience.

"I know, I don't want to either. But," he shrugs apologetically, "that's what they said. So we'll see you back out here in thirty minutes. We're just going to be behind the curtain."

The general babble of voices and movement of bodies tells me it's time to get up and suddenly I can't wait to move. I head for the bathroom and slip into a stall, so relieved to be free of that intensity for just a few minutes.

I ground and center myself, imagining a purple bubble of light surrounds me. Breathe in. Breathe out. Whew. Okay. I step out of the stall and up to the sink, wash my hands, splash some cold water onto my wrists. My pulse returns to normal. *God.*

I step back out into the melee and feel a sharp surge of joy as I make my way back to my seat and sit down.

"So are you a big fan of Eric Black?" the lady from seat 13 asks me.

I shake my head. "No. I'm a *huge* fan."

"He's wonderful. I've been coming to his concerts for a while now. So what do you do?"

"I'm, uh, a writer."

"I love books. I've always wanted to be a writer but, well, I can't start something like that now. I'm too old."

"Oh." I want to help her. Help her to feel the way I do right now. Help her to see that everything is all right. "It's *never* too late to start."

"Oh, I couldn't do that. But I do love reading. It gives me almost as much enjoyment as writing would." Another sigh. "What authors do you read?"

I rattle off a list that includes everything from Jane Austen to Dan Brown.

"That's quite the variety. What genre do you write in?"

"Right now I'm working on a romance."

"Oh! That must be wonderful. What's your name, dear?" the woman asks as the last of the house lights fade out. "I want to keep a lookout for when you're a famous author."

I turn to her, my eyes wide. This is a sign from the universe. "My name's Vicky Waverly."

And the music starts up again.

✧ ✧ ✧

MORE SWEAT DRIPS down Eric's face and there's a pause as he towels it away, takes off his suit jacket, drapes it over the edge of the piano and pushes up his sleeves, revealing the muscles of his forearms.

All at once, I want to just rip all my clothes off. Dance naked on top of the piano, then just lie there and feel these sweet vibrations move through me.

"Take it off! You're hot!" I hear a voice scream out. I turn and look. It's that same woman from five rows back.

Oh God. I'm mortified. I bring a hand up to my face and cast my eyes down. What if he thinks I made such a crass statement? Never mind the fact that I was actually *thinking* the very same thing.

Eric lifts his fingers from the keys. "Pardon me?"

There's dead silence.

"Really. I didn't hear you," he says. "Can you repeat that?"

Her tone turns sheepish. "I said this show is great."

"Glad you're enjoying yourself." He grins and resumes playing. "This is the last number," he adds.

A sharp, sweet sadness surges through me. No. No. No. I don't want him to go. How can it be ending when it feels like it has only just begun?

But all too soon, it does. He exits stage left.

Cerise and I get up too. I guess I lost my opportunity. No, I'm not going to think about it like that. It was a beautiful evening. I just need to be grateful for what I *did* receive.

We head out into the lobby. I look around for Sylvia but don't see her. Guess she's already left.

Then I see Eric. He's sitting behind a table with Farley and the other musicians, and a cluster of people surround them.

They're signing autographs. Now's my chance.

But I don't move. I have something to figure out first. I dig out my iPhone. A few keystrokes and I'm staring at the definition of the word that's been nagging me all night:

Eucris by Geo. F. Trumper was a men's fragrance launched in 1912 that became very popular in the 1920s, 30s and 40s. Contains caraway and coriander; jasmine and lily-of-the-valley; sandalwood, oak moss and musk.

Why the heck would a word I've never seen before just pop into my head like that?

Whatever. The important thing right now is my story; my fingers brush the pages of my manuscript. I glance up. More people are leaving the lobby.

I've put everything I have into this story. Fallen in love with my characters and their 1940s world. What if Eric leaves before I can speak to him? Worse, what if he thinks I'm a complete idiot for writing it?

"I'm going over there. I want Farley's autograph." Cerise walks over before I can stop her.

I glance around again. Even more people are leaving.

So why am I just standing here?

But I feel compelled to just stay still. Almost as if something is telling me not to move, even though that's the last thing I want to do.

Meanwhile, I watch as the last few people leave.

I see Cerise talk to Farley, who's standing beside her instead of behind the signing table, and they're snapping a picture together.

The signing table's pretty much empty except for Eric now, who's scribbling his signature on his latest album for the older lady from seat 13.

I really should go over to Farley and intervene on Cerise's behalf. But just as I'm about to tap her on the shoulder, I hear a voice behind me.

"Farley, you got the last of those CDs? We need to pack them up and load them onto the bus."

I turn. So do Farley and Cerise. Eric's still chatting with the older lady.

I watch a guy in a Taylor Guitars T-shirt and faded, torn jeans stride into the lobby carrying a beat-up cardboard box. He's such a contrast to Eric's polished,

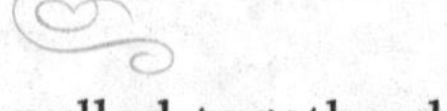

pulled-together look.

My heart skips a beat. I should've guessed. Where there's smoke, there's...er, where there's Farley, there's McCloud.

The cardboard box looks pretty heavy, judging from the way McCloud's biceps are bulging. The box doesn't look so hot, though; in fact, it looks like it might have been driven over by a steamroller *and* a Mack truck.

A furrow of concentration is on his brow as he sets the beat-up box down with a thud on the signing table and starts stacking the unsold CDs in neat piles inside.

McCloud sees me and Cerise and gives a polite nod. "Hi."

My heart plummets. "Hi," I reply. Guess he doesn't remember me. Then again, what did I expect?

"You sure that'll hold together, man?" Farley raises a brow as he leans down to pick up two much newer looking boxes and set them beside the one McCloud's filling.

"Yeah, yeah, it'll be fine." McCloud puts the last of the CDs into his box and shuts the lid. "This one just got a little bounced around in transit, is all. It'll hold together."

"If you say so," Farley says as he stacks the two other boxes on top of the one McCloud's holding.

"Ooof." McCloud adjusts his grip to accommodate. Dang, he must work out. I can't help myself as my eyes stray to his arms again.

McCloud lifts the three boxes and is in the process of pivoting away from the table when all at once, there's a tearing sound and a crash and the entire contents of the beat-up box is now on the floor.

McCloud looks down in some surprise. "Well, that didn't work like I thought."

"Oh my gosh. Here, I'll help." I immediately crouch down and reach for a few of the CDs.

He stoops down too and smiles at me. "Thanks." That Ivory soap and clean laundry scent of his drifts my way. Mmm. I'd totally forgotten about that.

He takes the CDs I hand him and places them in one of the other boxes. Then he pauses, cocks his head and says in an undertone, "Do I know you?"

"Um, well, I was a—"

"You guys need help?" Eric calls, looking over at us before handing the signed CD back to the older lady, who smiles and thanks him.

"Nah, we got it," McCloud says over his shoulder before swiveling his head back around, meeting my gaze. Those emerald eyes glint with a bit of something—mischief? I feel a zing. Uh-oh.

"You were what?"

"Oh, um." I feel myself blushing. "I was a volunteer for the Jeggs back in March. I, uh..." I concentrate on picking up the last few remaining CDs and hope he doesn't remember.

It's too late. "You were that driver who got us lost! I remember now."

"Yeah, well," I mutter, "sorry about all that."

"Hey, that's a stressful situation. And just so you know, we made it on time to that high school."

He reaches out to take the last few CDs from me and our fingers brush. Suddenly, that same urge that I first felt back in March, when I wanted to hug him, surges through me. I realize that I'm still holding onto

the CD. So is he.

"What's your name?" His voice is almost a whisper.

"Oh, uh...Vicky."

"Vicky," he repeats, holding my gaze a little longer than necessary. "Nice to see you again."

"You too." I clear my throat and straighten up. "Um, there you go." I release my grip on the last CD and his warm fingers fall away from mine.

He stands too, then opens his mouth as if to say something more to me. Before he can, Farley cuts in. "Come on, McCloud. We need to go. I'm starving."

McCloud clears his throat. Glances at me. Pauses. Then says, "Thanks again."

Shot down. "You're welcome."

He repositions the beat-up box on top of the other two. "Okay, Farley, let's go."

Cerise comes over to me and motions to the coat check. "Maybe we should get our jackets, huh?"

"I will in a minute. First, I have to give my story to Eric."

"But there's no one here."

I whip my head around. She's right. That older lady's gone. And so is Eric.

What? No!

Damn it. I shouldn't have wasted all that time talking with McCloud. My story will never see the light of day, and I'll never get his signature on this album, either. My mouth goes dry and I feel my palms get sweaty.

I hear a faint squeak and glance around. Oh! There he is, way down at end of the hallway. I try to look casual and unconcerned as I do an awkward run-walk toward him. Maybe I can make it. He's just about to go through the door.

But what if he laughs at me? The story? (Or thinks I'm a crazy stalker-fan?)

Too late for regrets and fears now because he turns toward me. Releases the door handle.

I increase my pace and close the distance, CD liner notes in one hand and my manuscript in the other.

The door closes with a soft click.

I exhale.

He shifts so that he's standing in front of the door. Right beside me.

Come on brain, work. "Sorry. I don't mean to bug you but..."

He looks at me with those caramel brown eyes. Smiles. "No problem."

I think I might faint. "Great show tonight."

"Thank you."

"You know, that song of yours on your latest album, um, really inspired me so I, uh, I wrote a story about it." With a shaking hand, I extend the manuscript to him.

"That's great. Except I..." He looks at me, then away, then back again. A pained expression—Worry? Confusion?—flits briefly across his face. "...don't have time to read this right now."

I gnaw my lip. Guess that's it, then. Except he doesn't move. Neither do I. The blood pounds in my ears. I hold my breath.

He clears his throat and shifts his weight.

So.

Much.

Silence.

I see his brow clear, as if he's come to some sort of conclusion, and he visibly relaxes. "Actually, meet me across the street at the Hilton bar in twenty minutes. I'd be happy to take a look at your story." He takes the manuscript, tucks it under his arm, then walks out the door.

✧　✧　✧

"CERISE, CERISE!" I'M lightheaded as I fumble for my jacket. "Did you hear? Did you see? I mean, I just—Eric just, that is, he—I...we...across..."

"Vicky?" Cerise finishes putting on her coat. "Are you okay?"

I grip her arm. "You have to come with me."

"Of course I'm coming with you. We're going home."

"No, no. We're going to the bar."

"You don't drink."

"I know, but Eric invited me. Please. You have to come with me. I'm afraid I might do something really stupid if you don't."

✧　✧　✧

AS CERISE SITS beside me drinking a glass of white wine, I clutch my Coke with lime, stirring the ice around and around in the glass with the straw. I can't breathe. Can barely think straight.

"Hi there."

I look up. The indirect lighting lends a softness and warmth to Eric's features and our surroundings. He settles onto the stool beside mine and a sense of

62

déjà vu washes through me so strongly that it leaves me dizzy.

By the time he pulls out the manuscript and sets it on the bar, the feeling's gone.

"Hi," I say. It comes out all breathy. He doesn't seem to notice my delayed response.

"Want anything?"

I lift my almost-full Coke glass.

He nods, then orders himself a glass of red wine, takes a sip. "So." He hefts the thick manuscript. "I only got as far as the title. But now I'm going to give this a look."

I gnaw my bottom lip, but nod. *Don't hate it. Please.* I try not to stare, but I can't help stealing covert glances at him as he reads the first page, then the second and the third, his elbows resting on the polished wood, his hair, I notice, slightly damp. Did he just shower?

Then I see it. A small smile that spreads into a grin across his face.

"You know..." he says, looking thoughtful. "That song..."

And then, all at once, he starts humming the melody.

Oh. My. God.

His gaze meets mine and I can't help myself—I start humming too. And this may sound crazy, but I swear I feel *something* pass between us.

He stops humming abruptly. "So what inspired you to write the story?"

I fiddle with the cuff on the sleeve of my dress. "The whole thing just unfolded in my mind, you know?"

But it's like he hasn't heard me. "Your dress..." He frowns. "Where—" He swallows. "Where did you get it?"

"Ordered it online."

"Oh." He blinks. "Right, right." He clears his throat and turns his attention back to the page.

Did he sound *sad*? Nah. It's just my imagination running away with me. Yet again.

"Nice. This story is very nice."

"Thank you."

"No, really. This is awesome." He looks back up at me.

I blush.

"You know, it's getting late. But I want to finish reading this; can I give you my feedback later? What's your email?"

Wait. What? Did Eric Black just... *Ahhhh*! Yes he did. I will not hyperventilate. I will not. I will not. I take a deep breath and scrabble for the pen and paper I always keep in my purse and scribble down my address.

He pockets it. "I'll email you."

"Thank you! Oh! One other thing?"

"Sure."

"Can I get your autograph?"

"Sure." He takes the CD and uncaps a black marker that he pulls from his suit jacket.

"What's your name?"

"Vicky."

"With an i or a y?"

"Y."

The marker moves across the glossy cover with a flourish as he signs his name and writes: "Enjoy the music, Vicky!"

Then he leans in.

Oh God. Is this happening?

I freeze.

And watch, almost out-of-body, as he puts his hands on my shoulders and presses his cheek against mine. *Ahhhh! If this is a dream, please, please don't wake me up.* My eyelids flutter closed.

His stubble scratches against me as he gives me a very enthusiastic air kiss. First on one side, then the other, before he releases me.

Dazed, all I can do is sit there, with my arms hanging limp and awkward by my sides, as he puts the album back down on the bar. "Thank you," I whisper, and I realize I'm trembling.

There's a lingering pause.

"Well, I have to go now." He glances at his watch and slowly gets up from the stool. "Have a good night." He lifts a hand and waves as he turns and walks away.

"You too." I wave back, then turn to Cerise, about to open my mouth.

"You can freak out in the car," she whispers.

Chapter Six

"Y OU HAVE TO let me know ASAP when he emails you. And every word you say." Cerise looks at me with a mock-stern expression as we're eating brunch at Smitty's the next morning.

I'm so tired. I didn't fall asleep until 2 a.m.

I blink and nod, slowly slicing into my waffle and taking a bite. *Mmmm, waffles.* I chew and swallow before speaking. "Don't worry, I will. But I hope he doesn't forget about me."

"I don't think he'll forget about you, Vicky." Cerise spears a slice of melon. "After all, he asked for your email. It's crazy what happened to you last night."

"Not crazy. Just fate. Plus a little help from my angels, maybe."

"Speaking of help, I've been doing a little rooting around on ol' Eric."

"*Ol'* Eric?"

"Gotta call him something that keeps him in perspective." She fixes me with a knowing look. "*Human,* in other words."

I mutter into my juice glass.

She points at me with her fork. "Did you know he did a cover of a song by Tom White? It's one of his gold singles."

"Eric's or Tom's?"

"Both. It became a hit for both of them."

"Makes sense. Same genre."

"True. But then I found this." She slides her phone across the table. I look down at it. There's a black and white photo of a man and woman, their arms around each other, looking adoringly into each other's eyes. It's from a newspaper article, dated April 2, 1946.

I read the cutline:

Jazz sensation Tom White and his new bride, Sarah.

But it's not the photo that gives me chills. It's what she's wearing.

A cherry-print dress. The exact same pattern as mine.

❖ ❖ ❖

SO I'VE BEEN compulsively checking my email twice a day for the last three days. Yeah, that might be a tad much, considering the novel is 109 pages and I only gave it to him three days ago. I mean, who knows how fast he reads? But I can't help my eagerness. I *so* want to know what he thinks of me—er, *it*.

I mean, he always replies to fans on social media so was I wrong to assume he'd reply to me via email? Well, I might as well do something useful for my career, so while I'm at it, I send Sylvia Washington a copy of the story.

❖ ❖ ❖

You tweeted! June 1, 8:55 a.m.
@ericblackmusic Hey Eric! Love to know your
thoughts on my novel! Thx.

@sylviawashington and 50 others have favor-
ited this.

✦ ✦ ✦

I'M LEAVING MY temp job the next day when my
phone vibrates and strains of Eric Black's version of
"It's Only a Paper Moon" start playing. I snatch up the
phone. It's a 905 area code. I don't know anyone in
Toronto...

Wait. Wait. Toronto? Oh my God. Maybe Eric
finally read the rest of my novel and is calling me!
(Never mind that he actually doesn't know my phone
number. Who needs coffee or chocolate when you're
addicted to drama?)

Even so, I wipe my sweaty fingers on my jeans
before hitting the talk button. "Hello?"

"Is this Vicky Waverly?"

Damn. It's a woman's voice. But hey, it *could* be
his assistant. *No, Vicky. Get with the program.*

"This is Susan Wright, head of the acquisitions
department at DiscoveryHearts Publishing. I'm Sylvia
Washington's boss."

"Yes?"

"We want to publish *Lyrics of Love*."

"*Seriously?*"

"Yes. We'll email you the contract, you can review
it, sign it and email it back and then we'll go from
there. Do you have any questions?"

"Uh..." I clear my throat. "I mean no. No, I don't."

"Great. We look forward to working with you. And congratulations!"

That afternoon, I check my email and find the contract. It's 50 pages long and overflowing with legalese.

I skim the document: royalty shares, rights licensing... Yadda, yadda. My eyes glazing over more quickly than a snowball in you-know-where. Well, I'm sure it's all standard, pat legal stuff.

I scroll to the bottom of the document and electronically sign it.

I bite my lip and stare at what I've just done.

It's official. I'm now a real author.

❖ ❖ ❖

From: <u>vicky.waverly@mail.com</u>
To: I don't even know your email address, Eric Black

Damn you, Eric Black!

I'm forced to write imaginary emails to you because it's been almost two months now and I haven't heard a single word back from you. Argh! I know you're a star but why the hell would you say something and then do nothing? I thought you were being real with me. But maybe I was stupid to think you'd actually read it—because I mean, who am I to you? No one. I guess I was just deluding myself into thinking you actually cared. About my art, at least. What's worse—I can't seem to get you out of my mind. This is crazy. No, wait. I'm probably crazy. But hey, at least I have a publishing contract. At least that one dream still came true.

Holding a grudge,
Vicky

✧　✧　✧

You posted on Eric Black's wall:

Hey Eric! Happy Canada Day! Hope you're having a good July 1 long weekend. Just wondered if you'd finished reading my novel yet?
Thank you. ☺ Vicky

Sylvia Washington likes this.

Eric Black commented on your post at 8:47 p.m. today.
Will get to your story soon. Been super-busy. ☺

You and *Sylvia Washington* like this. *You* and *Sylvia Washington* commented on this reply yesterday at 4:02 p.m:

Thank you, Eric. ☺

✧　✧　✧

I YAWN AND stretch as sunlight filters through the blinds the next morning. I drift into wakefulness, push my hair away from my face, and my fingers brush my pillow. It's damp. Like I've been...crying?

I sit up. Bits and pieces of a dream come back to me. A round, shining lake. Eric Black, wearing a beige suit, is drowning in the center of the lake, struggling, treading water but getting tired, so tired. *Sorrow. Pain.*

Then McCloud bursts onto the scene, riding a horse, his face obscured by a helmet. He's shouting, but I can't hear him. Then Eric disappears in a tidal wave.

A gray heaviness settles through me even as I push back the covers and get up. Have to get dressed. It's past 9:00. I pull on my jeans and T-shirt, wondering why I feel so sad when it was just a dream.

Why would my subconscious make up something so sad? Besides, I've never seen Eric wearing a beige suit. I reach for my dream dictionary underneath my dream journal and thumb through it. Hmmm. Looks like seeing a lake means unexpected events could happen and that I need to control my emotions. I'd say that's valid at this point.

I head to the kitchen and make myself some blueberry tea. I take a sip.

But something's still niggling at me. So I turn on my laptop and pull up Eric Black's Facebook page.

I have to refresh it twice before it sinks in.

This can't be real. Can't be true. I blink and look again.

But it's all too real. I feel a cold chill all over.

Eric Black updated his status. Posted 35 minutes ago:
Rest in peace, little sister...I love you... January 3, 1991-July 3, 2014.

That dream. My God.

I stare at the posted photo of Eric and his sister, the truth sinking in.

My chest heaves and I feel a fresh wave of pain as I stare at the photo, Eric's arm slung casually around his sister's shoulder, huge smiles on both their faces.

The urge to hold Eric suddenly surges through me. I want to wrap my arms around him and feel his tears, heal his pain; be strong for him; be kind to him; show him all the kindness and consideration that he showed me on that May night months ago.

To take his heart and pour it full of love and light once more, to whisper in his ear, "Just cry, just cry, it's okay. I know it hurts. I know, I know." Run my fingers through his hair, stroke his forehead, rest my cool cheek against his flushed one and just hold him.

Just like I had before.

Huh?

I shake my head and look around, bleary-eyed, wiping away the tears on the back of my hand even as I uncurl myself from the fetal position on the couch. That photo.

That dream. My heart hammers in my throat. Wait. I sit bolt upright. He was wearing a beige suit in that photo. And in my dream.

My skin erupts in goose bumps. There must be something metaphysical going on here.

I study the picture of him and his sister in front of me, and my fingers find their way to the keyboard. I say a quick prayer to Archangel Gabriel for clear communication, and begin to type a post onto his wall.

Oh, Eric, I'm so sorry to hear about your loss.

I bite my lip. I don't want to sound too depressing. I take a breath and with it, come new words:

May you find strength, peace and reassurance.

There. That's better.

I hit enter, and it pops up underneath the photo, the very top slot above 200 other people's condolences. I flick through their comments—people relating how they lost fathers, mothers, brothers, sisters; all his fans telling him to be strong, to hang in there; that it'll get better. God. Would he even read any of this? Would he even want to?

Suddenly, I feel incredibly selfish. Here I am, feeling all excited about our connection, when all he probably wants to do is curl up in a ball and die.

This is probably the worst day of his life.

❖　❖　❖

"NOW THAT YOU'VE signed the contract and sent us the final draft of your manuscript, we can talk about the cover art," Sylvia says. "I've been talking it over with my boss. We'd like to try to get Eric Black to pose as the hero for the cover, since he inspired the hero of your story. That's part of why we love your story and want to publish it. It's great marketing—a very unique cross-genre merging that both book readers and Eric's fans will love. It'll boost your book sales and his record sales, too."

"Besides," she continues, "the executive publisher knows a few people in the music industry in Toronto, so she can try to get permission from Eric's record company."

Sylvia pauses. "Since we're just a boutique e-publisher, we can't really afford to hire a model to pose as the heroine... But if *you're* the model and take care of most of the shoot expenses, then we can focus the majority of our money on obtaining the license to use Eric's likeness. We're not sure how much our budget's going to be, but don't worry, we'll definitely chip in some to help you with the shoot costs." She laughs. "What do you say?"

Oh my God. Shame fills me. I can't do that. I can't be on the cover. Oh God. What would people *think* of me? They'd think I was crazy. Insane. And worst of all, *pathetic*.

But so what?

Because suddenly something ticks over in my mind and I can see everything so clearly. Yes. This isn't about shame or what others think. It's about the art. It's about...revolutionizing the fiction industry. (Okay, *that's* a bit of stretch, but I love to think big!)

It's about doing the art justice, bringing it to life; it'd be like, being an actress, taking on the role... And what's more, this is clearly a sign from the universe. Okay, that probably sounds crazy but maybe, just maybe, it means I'm meant to go to Toronto and work with Eric. That there's a larger reason for all of this.

A delicious shiver slides down my spine. "Oh my God! I'd love to!" Now that I'm temping, I can at least afford the plane ticket out there. I can cash out my retirement savings to pay for the rest—I mean, how can I afford not to? Because using my savings would be an investment in my career and in my art that's sure to pay dividends.

"Perfect. We'll talk soon, then."

✦　✦　✦

You tweeted! 5 seconds ago.
@ericblackmusic My publisher wants to hire you

to be on my book cover. Pls let me know ASAP. Thnx!

@ericblackmusic replied to your tweet.
@vickyfangirl ☹ I'm sorry, Vicky. It's hard to arrange a shoot with my crazy schedule.

I resist the urge to hurl the laptop across the room and shake my head at myself. I do this all the damn time—become ridiculously optimistic about something that's impossible. I guess I let Sylvia's cover idea get my hopes dangerously high.

I just need to cut my losses and be grateful. Yes. *Grateful.* I grind my teeth. Because without Eric's inspiration in the first place, I wouldn't have the story at all. *Yes.* I force myself to smile at the computer screen. I need to channel my inner Pollyanna and be thankful for that small kindness and forget the fact that he didn't even email me the feedback he'd promised, either.

I mean, he's way too busy giving concerts and making albums to even think about me. How ridiculous to think he'd give me more than the time of day.

But hey, I have the perfect cure to forget about this whole fiasco.

The Taylor Swift concert in Saskatoon.

❖　❖　❖

"SO FANS ON Taylor's website say there's this extra-special exclusive party after the show, reserved for the most dedicated, committed, faithful Swifties, handpicked by Taylor's mom and her staff."

"Uh-oh. I know what that means." Cerise gives me

a knowing look. "I saw those Post-It note affirmations about meeting Taylor that you put on the bathroom mirror."

I cross my arms. "Please don't look at me like I'm a crazy fangirl. I mean, sure, I tend to get carried away, I admit it. But come on. I really want to meet her. What's wrong with a few affirmations? It's positive thinking. The universe is listening, after all. Besides, affirmations totally work. I mean, look what happened at the Jeggs! I was this close…"

Cerise rolls her eyes. "No disrespect to the universe and all, but don't say I didn't warn you."

"I know. After all the disappointments with Eric Black, you think I should stop giving in to this wild-eyed enthusiasm. But to quote Emily Dickinson, 'Hope is the thing with feathers that perches in the heart and sings and never stops at all.' You might call it stupidity or naiveté. I call it optimism. Because we create our reality, after all."

Cerise picks up her suitcase. "Well, let's get creating, then."

Yes. I'm going to be one of the chosen few, the hallowed faithful, a dedicated servant to bow at the altar of all things Swift. Yes. This is the perfect way to meet her. Poetic, and beautiful, and full of magic. It will be amazing and incredible.

After all, a series of magical events had unfolded when I'd given Eric Black my *Lyrics of Love* story, so I'm certain I'll have that same luck being able to meet Taylor at her concert.

What's more, it would be so empowering to know that I'd created something just by thinking about it, just by believing in it hard enough.

We're so alike—we share the fairytale idealism, the sweet nature, the creative endeavors. We both love cats, the East Coast, watermelon-flavor Sour Patch Kids, glitter, shopping in antique stores, sparkly chandeliers, preppy guys, and being dramatic...

We could totally be best friends.

Taylor understands me. Completely and totally. More important, she's there for me through her music. My loyalty to her is rock solid.

On top of that, I read my horoscope for the day of the concert. *Plans you make will be met with certain success. And a proposition you envision will come to light.*

This erases my final doubts.

As Cerise and I pack my car, loading up our dreams along with our luggage, she helps me stuff my sparkly purple ball gown into the back seat.

After all, wearing a prom dress is the best way to get noticed in a sea of 30,000 other Taylor fans.

We drive the three hours to Saskatoon, cranking up Taylor for the ride there, chatting about her, speculating on her love life and ooooh-ing over her awesomeness.

We check into the hotel and get room 213, a sign if I ever saw one. (Because 13 is Taylor's favorite number.)

Carefully putting my ball gown into the closet and stashing my handmade sign, complete with glitter glue, reverently in the corner, Cerise and I head downtown to try to find the arena where Taylor will be playing the next day. One less thing to stress about the day of.

Except we make more and more wrong turns. Was

this city designed by aliens? There are so many U-turns, clover-leafs and one-way streets that my brain feels like a pretzel—with extra salt. So, tired and even more annoyed, we blame aliens and give up, deciding to split cab fare to the show instead.

At three o'clock the next afternoon, the cabbie drops us off at Gate 1 and we hop out. The gates doesn't open for another hour but already the line's almost a block long. We take our place at the end and I crane my neck. Maybe Taylor's mom will magically appear. No. I need to just let it go. I force myself to stop thinking about it.

Time ticks by. I shift from foot to foot in the July heat. Maybe it was a bad idea to get here *so* early. Too late for regrets now, though.

At last. The gates have opened up and the line starts to move.

We inch closer to the front entrance.

I see a woman go by with a big, professional camera and a tag that reads MEDIA around her neck. She stops. Looks at me.

"Big fan?" she says. "You have by far the best outfit here. Do you mind if I take a picture of you for our Facebook page? Your dress exactly matches our station colors."

"Awesome! Sure!"

I eagerly jump out of line and pose for her, holding my sign aloft and grinning as she clicks the shutter on her camera.

This will all be worth it. Yet another sign from the universe.

"So what made you decide to wear a dress like this?"

"You know her song *Starlight*?"

She nods.

"Well, these sparkles are like starlight, and this gown reminds me of what a duchess would wear, because she talks about that in the song."

"Enjoy the show! I hope she notices you."

I almost skip back to my place in line. The good stuff is flowing in. See? When you believe, stuff happens. I knew it!

As we move through the gates, I see people all around smiling at me when they notice my dress and the *Starlight* song lyrics I got Cerise to write down my arms.

I'm already getting noticed. It's working! Why else would the universe give me these signs and confirmations?

I make my way with Cerise to our seats, and after putting down my sign, decide to check out the merchandise table. After discovering they just sell T-shirts, not the tour jackets or Keds I'd been hoping for, I head down to the lower arena level that gives me a perfect view of the stage.

Lifting my skirts so I don't trip and fall flat on my face, I slowly descend the stairs. (Hehe. I feel sort of like a princess.) As I walk by two guys with TEAM SWIFT T-shirts and all-access passes around their necks, one says to me, "Great dress!"

"Thanks!" I grin. I should wear prom dresses more often. Maybe it's the secret to get guys to notice you.

"Can we trade?"

I laugh. "Sure!" *If you give me your pass so I can meet Taylor, that is.*

But they just keep walking. Hmmm. I wonder if

those guys were in the same room as McCloud and Taylor when she was writing that one song...

Now at the arena railing, I stand there for a while in reverent silence. I remember Taylor's DVD documentary and the amazed, awe-filled expression on her face when she did her first headliner tour to her first sold-out crowd. How she had finally seen the realization of all her dreams. So inspiring. I want to inspire people that way. I want to give that amount of love to that many people.

I want to be just like Taylor.

Finally, I head back to my seat and the show begins.

At long last! At the start of the first opening act, I jump up and start dancing, determined to be on my feet for every act and every number. Because that way, I was sure to get the coveted shoulder tap that meant my dreams would come true. All I have to do is put out the effort.

By the beginning of the third opening act, my feet begin to feel a little sore and I feel a headache developing. I ignore all that and keep dancing. I have to keep at it.

In the 15-minute pause before Taylor takes the stage, my calves start cramping, and I'm forced to sit down.

Just then, a girl in a Taylor T-shirt approaches me. Oooh! This is totally my moment. My heart pounds and I hold my breath. All my effort might be about to pay off.

She says, "I wish I had the courage to wear an outfit like yours."

What? Those are not the words I wanted to hear.

How could she not be asking me if I want to go meet Taylor? I blink at her, forming my lips into an absent smile, too distracted by what she didn't say to fully register what she did.

She walks away, unacknowledged.

I'm a complete idiot. What sort of duchess would snub that beautiful gesture? It's too late for a do-over.

And then 30,000 people start screaming. The red velvet curtain onstage slowly rises. And Taylor's right there—outlined by backlighting as the familiar opening beats of her latest number-one song hit me.

It's like some other force takes over my body. I start jumping up and down, screaming out each line as loudly as I can. I'm really here! Singing along with Taylor merely a football field away.

The next few songs pass in a blur of vivid red lights and pulsing beats. My screams rise above everyone around me.

Don't they love Taylor too? And if not, why did they come? Come on, people, you're not in church! Get crazy!

I ignore their lack of proper enthusiasm and keep screaming song lyrics, because suddenly, I don't care what anyone else thinks of me. Even though my legs and feet are starting to ache from the hour-plus I've been dancing on this concrete.

I press a hand to my chest, chanting the words along with her and feeling to the very core of my soul that deep desire and longing to truly know her. Oh, meet-and-greet people, where *are* you?

I take a moment to sit down in a lull right before her very last number and catch my breath. It's only then that I remember Cerise is up on the concourse in

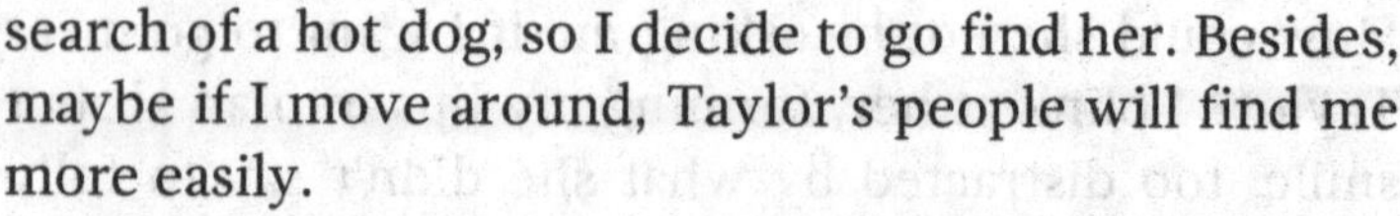

search of a hot dog, so I decide to go find her. Besides, maybe if I move around, Taylor's people will find me more easily.

I scoop up my sign and head for the stairs. My eyes flick to the faces I pass, seeing wide smiles on everyone who notices me. Reflexively I grin back.

As I near the top of the stairs, someone at the end of the row says, "You were amazing!" I smile, my hopes soaring once more. "Thank you!"

Finally I reach the top and spot Cerise, with a half-eaten hot dog in hand.

I feel a surge of panic and press my lips together, trying in vain to stem the flood of disappointment that suddenly overwhelms me.

Cerise looks a little worried, and hugs me. "I'm sorry. I know you wanted to meet her."

As I watch her finish her hotdog, the sadness creeps in. No one's coming for me, are they? No reward for all my hard work, all my effort. No happy, smiling Taylor staff with that special wristband at the ready, tapping me on the shoulder and saying, "Have you met Taylor before?" No Taylor saying, "Wow! Your dress is so pretty!" to me tonight.

Even though I know I'm acting irrational and ridiculous, I feel tears brimming.

None of it was real. And now there's a mustard stain on my dress.

Oh God. I was carried away by the delusions of hope and possibility.

Why, oh why, had I poured my heart and soul into all these pie-in-the-sky possibilities? Into every lyric she sang? Why, oh why, had I stood on that godforsaken cement for four hours straight? Why, oh why, do I keep deluding myself with all this fantasy?

What's wrong with me? Succumbing to all sorts of ridiculous nonsense, like voices in my head and visions. This is real life. When am I going to *learn*?

So I dry my eyes and straighten my spine. I'm just going to enjoy these last moments of the show, because no one's going to appear beside me as if by magic.

Except...except someone does. Two someones. Two little girls wearing Taylor T-shirts approach me shyly, their hair done just like Taylor's current style. "Can we get our picture with you?"

Huh? I blink at their hopeful, eager faces. And then I realize it's *me* they want to take a picture with.

They keep smiling. A surge of love fills me and I smile back. Because I know, in that moment, exactly what it's like to *be* Taylor Swift. To be a giver of dreams instead of a taker. To fulfill someone else's desires instead of focusing on my own selfishness. Maybe by not being given what I thought I wanted, I gained something even more valuable—a whole new perspective.

I do exactly what I know Taylor would have done. Put my arms around their shoulders. Smile. And say yes. Because what's better than meeting Taylor Swift? *Being* Taylor Swift!

Chapter Seven

AFTER A THREE-HOUR drive, Cerise and I are back in Regina and standing in line at Starbucks, so I can get over this post-concert jetlagged feeling.

"Grande chai with extra whip," the barista calls as she sets my drink on the pickup counter.

I balance the almost overfull cup in one hand while I clutch my phone in the other. I make my way over to the condiments table and as I set the cup down on the counter I notice the stack of CDs for sale. I pick one up to read the song list and notice the rainstorm logo at the bottom. I squint at the tiny type and my heart flutters.

Produced by Thundercloud Music.

I reach for one of the three remaining lids at the same time that a guy fitting three coffees into a carrying tray does.

He glances over at me. Smiles. Nice green eyes.

"Go ahead. I don't need it," he says.

Mmmm. Is that Ivory soap I smell?

"Are you sure? I don't really need a lid, either." I lean in a tad closer than necessary.

"It's all right."

I give my head a slight shake. Nope, not Ivory soap. Obviously, seeing McCloud's record label has me imagining all sorts of things.

"So you don't want the lid?"

"Oh, uh, yes. I do." I snatch it up a little quicker than necessary. "Thanks."

I pick up my chai and make a beeline for the exit, leaving the guy standing there, looking puzzled.

I'm just about out the door when my phone buzzes. I glance at it. Incoming email. Probably Cerise reminding me about her poetry slam this weekend.

I walk to my car and get in, put my chai in the cup holder and reach for my phone. I don't work this weekend, so I can definitely go. I'll just confirm her message now.

But...

It's not from Cerise at all.

It's from eblack@ericblackmusic.ca.

Damn it. I resist the urge to chuck the phone out the window. Why now? I can't read it. Maybe it's safer to never open it.

Yes. I could delete it.

Right here and now. End things before that whole crazy-obsessive cycle begins again.

If I learned anything from the Taylor Swift concert, it was that.

I look again, and in that brief moment of hesitation, I'm a goner. Because it sinks in. He got back to me. After all that wasted energy spent on doubt, fear and worry. He got back to me.

That little bird named hope starts to chirp in my heart.

Uh-oh.

A slow grin starts to spread across my face. He got back to me! I can feel excitement bubble up within me like too much champagne.

No, Vicky, no. Just delete it.

No, that's silly. Be logical, Vicky. It's just an email, not a bomb or a matter of life and death.

I take a deep cleansing breath.

It's only an email. I can do it. I can read it. I just need to be centered. Remain calm. Breathe. And do *not* have any expectations. I can't do that to myself so soon after Taylor's concert.

Click.

Loading...loading...loading...

It's just an email.

From: <u>eblack@ericblackmusic.ca</u>
To: <u>vicky.waverly@mail.com</u>
CC: <u>carltodd@ericblackmanagement.com</u>

Hey Vicky,

Loved your novel! You definitely have a flair for setting a scene—I could imagine everything so easily.

By the way, I talked to my manager about the shoot. He loves the idea. So I'd be available the 15th of August. Just contact him to make arrangements. I cc'd his email here.

Talk soon.

EB

I stare at the screen, the blood pumping through my veins at a ridiculously fast pace. I was right—he does appreciate my art! My heart speeds up.

No, Vicky. Calm down. Can't get myself emotionally involved in this. And he's not—obviously. Because he said, "contact my manager," not "call me." So of course this is strictly professional. Strictly. The focus is on bringing the art to life, not on getting to hang out with him.

So I very calmly start my car and head back to the apartment.

Now I need to find a photographer.

✧   ✧   ✧

I'M SITTING AT my doctor's office the following week for my annual physical and I'm flipping absently through an issue of *Canadian Living* magazine. What dresses are must-haves? Maybe I can find ideas for a new pair of sandals. Hmmmm. Ads, ads, ads. Flip. Flip. Ooooh, cute pair of sparkly jeans. Oh, and that's a great sundress.

Oh, okay here are great looks. A full five-page spread. Wow. Love that chiffon coral blouse...and that lighting...beautiful. Look at that doorway. Looks completely vintage, like an old hotel or...

Holy! That'd be perfect for the novel cover. The way she's leaning around the doorframe, smiling and looking all expectantly happy and excited, like she's just met the love of her life.

I glance around furtively. No one's sitting nearby. Would it be so wrong to rip out the...

"Vicky? Come on back, please."

I set the magazine back down on the coffee table and jump up. Saved from my about-to-incur-bad-karma move. "Sure."

Forty-five minutes later, I head back through the reception area on the way to the door. No need for a co-pay up here in the Great White North. (Gotta love free Saskatchewan health care.)

I glance over at the coffee table again. Yep, the magazine's still sitting there. Oh, what the heck.

I make a move toward the table and pick up the slightly tattered *Canadian Living* and walk up to the reception desk.

"Excuse me. There's a picture in here I'd like to take, and wondered if I could?"

"Oh, just go ahead and take the whole thing, hon." The silver-haired receptionist smiles at me.

"Awesome. Thanks."

I tuck it in my purse and head out the door.

I unlock the apartment door and head inside. Hmm, Cerise must be at work., I rip out the page and tack it to the fridge.

Hmmm. I wonder who took the photos for the spread? They're really good. I squint at the fine print at the bottom of the first page. Clothing provided by...blah, blah, blah... Ah yes. Here we are. *Photography by Jacques DuBois. Shot on location at the Gladstone Hotel, Toronto, ON.*

I Google his website. Yep, no doubt about it. He's *really* good. And—whoa! He's shot for *Vogue*. Both the British and American versions. No price listed, but hell, why not at least ask?

I mean, my story's my *baby*. Nothing's too good for it. Quality, quality, quality. It has to be...perfect. (There, I said it. I'm a perfectionist.)

To: jdubois@finefocusphotography.ca
From: vicky.waverly@mail.com
Subject: Photo shoot for book cover
Sent: July 20 at 1:34 p.m.

Mr. DuBois,

I found your photos in last May's Canadian Living *and am interested in hiring you for a photo shoot I'm doing in August for a book cover. What are your rates?*

Thanks very much.

Regards,
Vicky Waverly

To: <u>vicky.waverly@mail.com</u>
From: <u>jdubois@finefocusmedia.ca</u>
Subject: Re: Photo shoot for book cover

Hello Vicky,

What type of shoot are you looking to do? How many hours are you going to spend? Do you need models? How many photos do you need? What locations are you envisioning? I do charge extra for travel.

Best,
Jacques

To: <u>jdubois@finefocusmedia.ca</u>
From: <u>vicky.waverly@mail.com</u>
Subject: Re: Photo shoot for book cover

Jacques,

Thanks for your quick reply! It'd be probably a day-long shoot, at most. August 15th is the date I need. Don't need models. I am going to be one of them, as well as jazz singer Eric Black. I'd like to do it at the Gladstone Hotel where you shot that spread for Canadian Living.

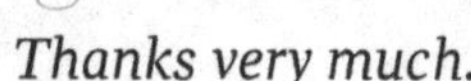

Thanks very much.

Regards,
Vicky

To: <u>vicky.waverly@mail.com</u>
From: <u>jdubois@finefocusmedia.ca</u>
Subject: Re: Photo shoot for book cover

Vicky,

Yes, that is fine. My day rate is $1,500. Is that feasible for you? Just to let you know, it's non-refundable and I require it upfront. Any additional expenses will be added onto that base price. By the way, I've worked with Eric Black before—I shot him for Chatelaine *a few years ago.*

I need to double-check that date and will get back to you ASAP.

Jacques

I nearly choke on my drink. $1,500? Well, since I didn't get an advance from the publisher, this shoot would pretty much use up the last of my savings.

But hey, $1,500 is really pennies compared to what I'm getting for that amount—Eric Black on the cover of my novel. It's an investment, not an expenditure. Gotta think like a CEO, here.

Besides...I feel a giddy wave of delight. This is bordering on ridiculous and impossibly coincidental. What are the chances? I go to my doctor's appointment, randomly flip through old magazines, randomly happen to like these photos, randomly discover he's a Toronto photographer, send him a message and then he *just happens* to have worked with Eric before?

I wouldn't have believed it if it hadn't happened to me. My skin erupts in goose bumps. It must mean the photo shoot is *meant to be*.

❖   ❖   ❖

"WELL, FOLKS, WITH that tailwind, we'll get you to the gate here in Toronto five minutes early," the pilot announces. Oooh. Landing early. The first good omen of this trip.

The plane glides to a stop and a familiar *ding*! has me fumbling to unclasp my seatbelt. I yawn. Ugh. Getting up early tomorrow is going to be brutal. But I'm doing it for the shoot, for my art. It's worth the pain. Besides, I have three whole days in town, so I'll have plenty of time to sleep after the shoot.

"The local time is three minutes to midnight. Have a pleasant stay in Toronto, or wherever your final destination may be."

I heave my purple carry-on and garment bag out of the overhead compartment and make my way out of the plane and into Pearson International.

Hello, Toronto.

Now I need to find a taxi, get to my hotel, and get some sleep.

❖   ❖   ❖

I YAWN AND groan before tossing the covers aside. Must. Get. Up. I jump into the shower, turn it to cold, which jolts me awake. Then I carefully get dressed, making sure the fragile vintage dress that I spent days tracking down is still wrinkle and lint free. Yep. Good to go.

I check my watch and stow a granola bar in my purse, too keyed up to eat anything now. I grab my rolling duffel with its extra change of clothes and a couple vintage props, then head down to the lobby.

Twenty minutes later, I'm at the door of the hair salon.

I jump out, pay the driver, then peek in the salon window. No one's here yet. I check my watch and chew my lip. It's almost 9 a.m. and I specifically told her I needed to start right away since the shoot starts at 10:30 a.m.

I feel a nagging sensation in my stomach. What if she doesn't show up? Oh, wait. I breathe out a sigh of relief. The lights are coming on now.

I see the girl unlock the door. She has colorful tattoos, a nose ring and orange hair. Did I book the wrong stylist for my vintage look?

She smiles at me as I step through the door. "Hi. You must be Vicky?"

"Yep."

"Great. Just come on back and we'll start washing your hair."

After my hair has been thoroughly washed and blown out, she goes about curling it. "This'll make your hair easier to style for the 1940s look you want."

"I still think it's amazing how you can create that look without me having to cut my hair."

She laughs around a mouthful of pins. "Yeah. That's what these five hundred bobby pins are for." She continues twisting my hair up and securing it with pins. "I love the 1940s. It was such a glamorous time."

But I'm not feeling glamourous at all. My butt's starting to go numb from sitting so long in one spot without moving. I glance at the clock. Crap. It's 10 a.m.

"My shoot starts at 10:30."

"Nothing like a tight deadline to build a fire under my ass." She laughs. "I work best under pressure."

Let's hope so.

She jams the last few bobby pins into my hair and I try not to wince with the pain. After all, what's art without a little suffering?

Twenty minutes later, the makeup's on. "Now for the finishing touch." She approaches with some sort of device that looks like a cross between a branding iron and some sort of dental tool.

She leans forward, opening the device's jaws.

I jerk my head back.

"Don't blink. Eyelash curler. There," she says. "All done. And now," she whips out a hand mirror. "Take a look."

I look at the face in the mirror. Who the hell is that woman? She looks totally hot! Whoa. It takes me a minute to find myself beneath the layers of eye shadow, eyeliner, lip liner and blood-red lipstick.

But that's the point, after all. I'm not supposed to look like me. "Perfect."

The stylist takes the black drop cloth off me and I hop up with a worried glance at the clock. 10:32.

I snatch up my purse from beneath the chair and speed walk over to the cash register.

"That'll be $86.47."

I grin as I punch in my PIN and then give her a fifty dollar tip. I don't care how much money it costs, because my dream is coming to life.

And that's worth any price.

◇　◇　◇

I SCURRY ALONG the sidewalk as fast as my chafing heels will allow while holding my hat with one hand and the roller duffel with the other. Funny how five blocks looks a lot shorter on Google maps.

Never mind. Out of breath, I tug open the door of the Gladstone Hotel. I'm here now. Only fifteen minutes late to my own photo shoot.

With any luck, Eric will forgive me.

I lug the heavy duffel up the stairs to the second-floor shoot location, pausing on each step. In a few more hours I'll have some lovely blisters.

But a thrill of awe and wonder overrides my foot pain as the realization sets in. I'm here at last. I've created this. Done this amazing thing pretty much all by myself. If I could high-five myself, I would.

Instead, I open the door.

Jacques glances up from the chair he's seated in. "Hello. Vicky Waverly?"

"Yes." I shake his hand, set the duffel down and then look around.

Eric's nowhere to be seen. "Has Eric contacted you? I think he's running late."

Jacques shakes his head. "No, he hasn't."

I glance at my watch. Twenty minutes after the scheduled shoot start.

Considering I was running late myself, I'm sure Eric has a good reason, too. He'll be here. He confirmed it last week via Facebook.

So I busy myself with smoothing down my dress and then adjusting the small oak table in the center of the room—the one Jacques had brought in for the shoot, as I'd specified.

I can't help running a finger along the smooth polished surface; at once, a sense of longing fills me.

"Oh you remembered!" I smile as sun glints off the small oak side table's shiny surface.

"I knew you loved it. So I bought it for our place," a man's voice says from over my shoulder.

I peer into the next room. "This is the perfect apartment. I love it. And I love you—"

"I will need to take some test shots." Jacques's voice startles me and the images fade from my mind's eye. "We might as well start now."

I shake my head and check my watch to cover my confusion. 10:55. "Okay." No reason to panic. That's only twenty-five minutes after the start time. It's Toronto. I'm sure traffic's crazy.

But why hasn't he emailed me? Or sent me a Facebook message? I double-check my phone. Nope. Nothing.

Damn it, I wish I'd made Cerise come with me. At least we could worry together. But no. My pride got in the way, so I decided to be all brave and go by myself. Take on the jobs of like, five different people. For one stupid cover.

God, what was I thinking? I blink rapidly. Maybe I *wasn't* thinking. Or maybe...

I start to pace. Back and forth. Back and forth. The suspense is killing me. And so are these heels.

Oh god, what will I say to him? Me. Alone in a

room with Eric Black. It's too good to be true.

Breathe. Just breathe. He actually has to show up first before I can freak out.

I inhale through my nose, still pacing. I glance at Jacques. No help there. He's done with his test shots now. And he hasn't moved. Except for his fingers, frantically texting.

Hmmm, I guess I could text Cerise... No. I have to talk myself off this ledge. I bring a nail up to my mouth but just in time, jerk my hand away. Must not. It'll ruin my manicure. I force myself to do more deep yoga-style breaths instead of chewing my nails.

Eric's forgotten, hasn't he? I feel nausea start to creep in. All that money. Oh God. I gnaw my bottom lip. All my effort. Such a huge waste.

He's a star, a public figure, for crying out loud. He didn't remember me and my silly little photo shoot appointment. This time my nail does find its way to my mouth. Screw the manicure.

I blink again, inhaling and exhaling. I need to be strong. In control of myself. I'm jumping to conclusions and I—

What was that?

My head jerks toward the door and my heart starts galloping again. Someone's actually coming? Yes. I definitely hear a rattling noise.

The door opens.

I jump as if electrocuted and rush forward, my hand extended toward...a blonde chick?

Wearing a tight, short pencil skirt and matching jacket. Carrying a garment bag.

"Hello there!" she says in a Slavic accent, grining at me and giving a little wave with her free hand. "I'm Zosia."

"Hey!" I find myself impulsively returning her smile. "Vicky."

Where's Eric? I open my mouth to tell her she's in the wrong place when he walks in behind her.

So who is this woman? His assistant? I ignore a twinge of jealousy. Of course he has an assistant.

As Eric steps into the room, with that smile and those eyes, though, all is forgiven. Hell, he could've been two hours late and I wouldn't have cared. Because all that matters is this moment. All my hard work. All my dedication to my art is about to come to fruition at last.

He looks at me, those caramel-brown eyes liquid with their intense sincerity. "I'm so sorry I'm late, Vicky. Forgive me. We got stuck behind some sort of police escort and I couldn't find my phone till just now, so I couldn't contact you. I'm really sorry."

I give a rather shaky laugh. "No problem." I wave my hands around the room, wishing my heart wasn't pounding so hard that I'm worrying it might burst from my chest. "Jacques and I were just going over some, uh, last-minute details." I grin brightly, glancing over at Jacques. He doesn't look up from his iPhone. Um.

Eric just nods. "Right, well, let's get to it then."

Zosia has put the garment bag on the table and seated herself on the spare chair.

I walk over to Jacques. "We're ready to go now."

He snaps to attention, shoves his iPhone in his Nikon bag and stands up. "So what I think is that you wish to create the type of shall we say, vintage vibe, no?"

"Yes." I nod. "Exactly." There's a reason he's done

Vogue covers. (See, hiring quality totally pays off.)

Eric nods too. "Whatever you need to do. You're the expert. Let me just put on my suit jacket here...."

Zosia, who had been calmly flicking through *Us Weekly*, looks up and gives him a 1,000-watt smile. Maybe she's his publicist. Or agent. Or something.

She unzips the garment bag and pulls out a pin-stripe charcoal-gray jacket and brings it over to Eric. "Here you go."

He takes it from her, sliding his free arm around her waist. Okaaay. Getting friendly with his— publicist? Assistant?

"Thanks, Zosia."

Agent? Producer? Or... girlfriend? I eye his hand on her hip again. A girlfriend, sure, I could see that. But girlfriends come and go. Like the seasons. Like melting snow. Like...like...

"Vicky, did you meet my wife?"

Not once, in all my obsessive article reading and interview watching, did he ever mention a wife! Ever. And surely he didn't just up and get married like, five minutes ago—did he? Maybe that's why he was late. Er, maybe not.

My gaze flicks to his left ring finger. Still nothing there. So that means no wife. What kind of married man doesn't wear a wedding band? (Okay, maybe that's a bit unfair. I'm sure there's a good reason.)

But from where I'm standing, there is no good reason.

Eric cocks his head. Zosia frowns, the skin above her brows puckering ever so prettily. And I realize my mouth is hanging open.

"Er, uh..." I clear my throat. "Sorry! I was um, er, I

mean, that is to say I uh..."

God. Stop floundering like a fish. This is strictly business, remember? I raise my chin. This is for the art. Be professional. Strong. So I manage a smile. "Yes, er, how nice. Congratulations!"

Zosia inclines her head. "Thank you—we've been married five years now." She slides her hand into Eric's.

Anger slices through me, closely followed by helplessness. "Oh, well, that's great." I spin on my heel and blink back tears.

Wife. Wife. *Wife*. A four-letter word. It'd be easier if he'd said he was gay.

"Yes." Zosia giggles, then smiles at me. I want to hate her. But somehow her smile's too genuine, her manner's too sincere, for me to do anything but surprise myself by smiling back.

Zosia helps Eric on with the jacket, brushing a stray thread off the lapel. "There," she murmurs. "Perfect."

It's when she gives him a quick peck on the lips that I think maybe I can hate her after all.

And then Eric turns to me. Zosia's right. *He* looks absolutely perfect. *The suit* looks absolutely perfect. Narrow lapels. Pinstripe. Exactly how I envisioned the hero of my story. My knees go weak.

Jacques takes me by the arm. "You sit here. And Eric, he sits there. At the table." Jacques frowns.

I take a deep, cleansing breath. *I will be strong. I will be stoic. I will get through this.* After all, I'm doing it for my art. I can't let my heart's desire override what's best for my art. And my publishing contract.

I go to the spot he points at on the floor, wobbling

only a little in my three-inch cherry-red heels.

"I need to test the lighting here." Um, isn't that what he was supposed to be doing when we were waiting around for Eric, instead of being glued to his iPhone? But who am I to question the mind of a creative genius?

Minutes tick by, marked by the constant click of the shutter release and Jacques's frown, just visible above his Nikon. I sit in silence, wondering if I should make small talk with Eric or if sitting awkwardly is just part of the deal.

After what seems like an hour but is probably only five minutes, Jacques's smile has replaced his frown. "Now, we start."

I snap into professional mode. "Great. So what I was thinking was, the hero—that's you, Eric." I glance over at him. He just nods. "The hero would be sitting on a chair with one arm draped casually over the back of it. And the heroine—that's me." I feel a blush creeping up my neck. What do they think of me for doing all this? They must think I'm crazy. Stupid. Acting out some sort of fantasy.

No. *I am a professional. It's my art. Just breathe. Focus.* "The heroine would stand behind him over—"

"No, no, no, no, no." Jacques is frowning again. "Just like before." He waves a hand. "Sit where you were before. That is what I feel is best for the portraiture."

"Oh, but you see, as the author of the story, I feel that the characters are best represented by—"

Jacques folds his arms across his chest.

Damn it. This is my shoot. Not his. I hired him. Who does he think he is, Mr. Best-Photographer-In-

The-World-Because-I-Shoot-For-*Vogue* or something?

"No." I almost scare myself at the vehemence in my voice. Crap. Eric's right there. I need to cool it.

I take a breath and try again. *Professional.* In a soft, ladylike tone. "Jacques, while I'm sure that from your point of view, the pose of the two characters makes sense, I feel that because it's my book and my characters, that the creativity that's going on here needs to be somewhat..." I clear my throat. "Collaborative." Now I'm the one who folds my arms.

Jacques's eyes narrow to slits and he points to his camera emphatically. "I am the photographer. Give me a chance. I know what I'm doing."

Fine. Fine! You know what you're doing but you won't bloody well listen to me. I glare at him, angrier at myself for backing down from a fight—as usual—than at him, now.

I grind my teeth and give him a curt nod. Damn avant-garde creative types. They have no sense of anything but their own vision. But who am I to talk?

Before Jacques can lift his camera again, Beyoncé's latest hit blares through the silent room. I tilt my head in Zosia's direction.

But it's coming from Eric's phone. Why isn't it classical? Or opera? Or, oh, I don't know, *jazz*, maybe?

Hello, reality check.

Eric shoots me an apologetic glance. "I'm sorry. I have to take this. It's my manager." I just nod. What am I supposed to do—say no?

I stare at the floor, doing my best to look like I'm not listening while actually straining to hear the conversation. I'm paying for every second, here. Might as well get the most from it.

But his side of the chat does nothing to enlighten me. All I can hear from the other person is the equivalent of a McDonald's employee talking through the speaker at a drive-through window. And I definitely don't want fries with that.

Eric ends the call and looks at me. "I'm really sorry, Vicky. I have to go."

Before we've even started the shoot? The universe obviously has a conspiracy against me. I grit my teeth. Be professional. Be calm.

"It's the George Stroumboulopoulos show. Apparently I have a taping there. I was supposed to be there ten minutes ago. Can still make it if I hurry." He stuffs his cell back into his suit jacket and checks his watch. "I'm sorry about what that means for your shoot, Vicky. But it's damn hard to reschedule with him—his people like to line things up way in advance."

"Oh."

I guess that's show biz. But my hands are trembling. I take a deep breath before extending my hand to shake his. "Thank you anyway for coming."

"No problem. Good luck with the project... Hey, you okay?"

I nod. "Just h-have something in my eye." I sniff and blink and rub at my mascaraed lashes.

"I'm sorry," he repeats. "Somehow my agent double-booked me." He shakes his head. "This Christmas album I'm in the middle of cutting has done crazy things with my schedule." He frowns, looking truly chagrined.

I try for a light breezy laugh. But I can't breathe. "Of c-course."

Eric picks up the garment bag, then strides briskly

out the door as he says, "I'll see you at home later, Zo. Bye, everyone."

As the door clicks shut, I hear a step behind me. I turn and jump. It's Zosia. My breath hitches as I inhale, willing myself to remain calm.

"It's not just about the shoot, is it, sweetie?"

I blink and shake my head.

She puts her hand on my shoulder and I tense up. How can she be so nice? So...human? But with her tiny compassionate gesture, I feel the last of my defenses slipping away and the tears spill over in earnest. I am such a failure. Pathetic. Delusional. She's so much better than I am. Eric totally deserves her.

"Can I give you a hug?"

I nod, numb.

I'm enveloped in a cloud of Chanel, but I clutch her like I'm drowning. It feels so good to be held—at least someone cares.

I sob into Zosia's tailored Donna Karan suit jacket as the words spill out of me. "But...but...but...he said yes." Sob. Sniffle. "I w-w-worked so hard. All, all those details. All that money and...and..."

"I know, I know... Just let it out," Zosia murmurs, patting my shoulder.

"Damn this whole stupid project. No, damn *me*, because I was stupid enough to think it might even work somehow. God. Back in Regina, I thought...I thought I had something! I thought because of the story... I poured everything I had into it. My heart. My soul. And now? Now there's nothing."

I squeeze my eyes shut, not even sure if she understands my babbling. Hell, I barely do. "I thought that he... I can't believe I was such an idiot...again."

Zosia murmurs and nods again. My sobs finally subside into hiccups. She pulls out a Kleenex and I blow my nose.

"Sweetie," she says, "you're all alone here in Toronto. So anytime you feel bad, you call me, no?"

"No." I manage a wobbly smile. "Er, I mean, *yes*. Thank you."

But as she leaves, the helplessness she'd held at bay comes crashing down around me again. I look around at the props, the empty chairs, the lingering feeling of failure—the knowledge that nothing went as I'd imagined, hoped or expected.

It's over. It can't be over. It's over. It can't be over. It's over. It can't be over.

Jacques turns to me, his mouth moving, but strangely, I can't hear him. There's this weird ringing sound in my ears, high-pitched and tinny, and my thoughts are racing. I need out. I need air. I need to think rationally. I stumble through the door and past the front desk. I discover I've burst out into the street, caught in the noonday throng of downtown Torontonians going about their lunch hour.

My eyes dart around as if searching for Eric. *No. Stop it, Vicky. Stop this obsessing. Be rational. He's gone. Back to his own life, his own schedule, his own deadlines, his own wife, damn it.*

Somehow, that knowledge just gives me fuel. I push upstream against the flow of humanity, my eyes darting around, my vintage hairstyle tumbling out of its pins. Yet another waste of money.

Why am I so obsessed with him? How has it come to this? It's like a drug. An addiction to him. I feel a sharp stabbing in my solar plexus.

And now I don't get a redo. It's over and all my hard work did *not* pay off. And I still have to pay off those bills. Worse, what do I tell Sylvia about all this? Argh! It's enough to make me want to throw myself in front of a bus.

Ah, here comes one now. It's—I squint at the digital read-out as it barrels through the green light—the 15A. I can't help entertaining the thought—for about five seconds. Hey, it could have its advantages. Give St. Peter a piece of my mind...learn to play the harp... All my problems would be solved.

Uh, no. I let out a snort of laughter at my thoughts. And with that laughter, at last, the weight finally lifts.

Silencing my inner drama queen by getting hit by a bus is not going to solve my problems or this situation. Maybe this isn't even a problem. Maybe it's simply a perception I need to change, need to heal, to understand, in order to move on, in order to create space in my life so that the best things possible can come into it. The best *man* possible. The best *art* possible. And it's going to start right now.

At Starbucks.

I pull open the coffee shop door and pause a moment, savoring, as always, the rich aroma of eau du coffeehouse—warm, sweet, deep and heady—the dark roasted coffee scent mixing with the latest green tea concoction, the squeal of steam as the baristas make foam for mochaccinos and caramel lattes, all topped off by the cacophony of friendly chatter and chairs scraping on the tiled floor.

Ah, pure heaven. I smile, feeling myself relax for the first time in days, as I join the end of the line. There's nothing in life that a hot drink won't cure.

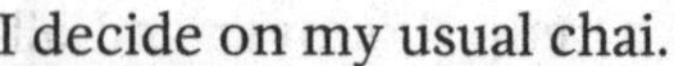

I decide on my usual chai.

The line proceeds slowly, which gives me more than enough time to think. (And rearrange my rat's-nest hair.) I'm tired of just reacting blindly to everything. I can't keep doing this to myself. I need to be strong. It's time to stand up and be a real woman. I shake my head. I need to start acting like the twenty-four-year-old that I am, even if I don't want to, even if it's scary.

I'm near the head of the line, so I start to pull out my wallet as the cashier looks my way. I find a wad of crumpled fives that I'd stuffed in my purse haphazardly that morning after I'd paid the cab. One of the blue legal tenders floats down to the floor, the rather dour face of Sir John A. McDonald looking balefully up from his undignified spot on the tiles.

I crouch down to retrieve it and almost knock heads with the man in line behind me who's somehow beat me to it. Hey! That's *my* money—oh, wait. He's handing it back to me. I shift my weight sheepishly. So he wasn't going to steal it. "Thank you." I study the man in ripped jeans and a faded T-shirt for a half-second longer.

He smiles. "You're welcome." And even though I know he's not him, I can't help but think fleetingly of McCloud.

As I hand the five to the harried girl behind the till, I fish out an extra ten-dollar bill and stuff it into the tip jar—I'm having such a bad day, she might as well have a great one.

I study the man for a half-second longer before I grab my drink and some sense and head for a table by the window.

I have business to attend to. I fish out my phone from my purse. The bile rises in my throat.

I take a breath. *Angels, universe, please give me strength.* I dial.

"Sylvia Washington."

"Sylvia, um, hi." There's a long pause. I can't do this. I don't want to do this. I have to do this. I'm sure they'll be able to work out some other sort of cover.

"Listen, um, the photo shoot with Eric Black, uh..." Come on, come on. I can do this. "It didn't pan out," I say as quickly as possible, kind of like ripping off a Band-Aid.

"I'm glad to hear that. Because DiscoveryHearts Publishing is now out of business."

"*What*? You must be joking. You guys have been around for a few years now. I thought... What about the contract I signed? The rights to the story, all of that?"

"Don't worry, they'll revert back to you. And, well, that's the nature of boutique e-publishers, you know. Overextending funds to try to gain sales and then going bankrupt for it. I'm sorry, Vicky."

I struggle to keep the bitterness out of my tone. "I'm sorry, too."

"Goodbye, Vicky."

"Goodbye, Sylvia. Thanks for believing in me, at least for a little while."

"Hey, it's a cute story. You could always just publish it yourself. Good luck."

The line goes dead.

I feel like I'm a zombie apocalypse survivor, gnawed on and then stomped to pieces by blank-eyed corpses.

With superhuman effort, I pull myself off the stool and head to the bathroom to splash cold water on my red, puffy eyes.

I survey myself in the mirror. Hey, things can't get any worse, right? Wasn't it J.K. Rowling who said something like rock bottom was a foundation that she built a new life upon? Well, hell, if she can do it, so can I. This is not the end of the world.

I straighten my shoulders. Try out a smile. It's not the end of my writing career, either.

With new resolve, I leave the bathroom, go back to my table, pull out my purse, rip out a sheet of notebook paper and uncap my pen.

I close my eyes for a minute and the noise of the coffee shop around me just falls away. Now focused, I open my eyes again and put pen to paper.

I inhale. *I'm not a victim.* Yes. I exhale. *I get to choose how I feel.* Because I've decided, right here and now, I'm going to win. Because I'm going to turn this whole mess into a piece of art. I'm going to be just like Taylor Swift.

I'm going to write a song.

I smile and lift my mug in a silent salute, imagining her and me bonding together over bad boys and broken dreams. Maybe even baking together— cupcakes with sparkly purple icing.

Life can throw stuff at me, but it doesn't matter how bad it gets. I'm going to write about it. I'm going to put myself into my art and maybe, just maybe, it'll resonate with others, too.

I poise my pen over the page. Imagine an ocean of songs just waiting to be tapped into. Imagine that all this pain has coalesced into crystal-clear art.

As I relax and tune in, a melody takes shape. It gets louder. More insistent. The words have a cadence and rhythm all their own, encapsulating my anger, my fear, my broken-heartedness.

Got the chorus.

I grin.

The melody and the words come faster now, and my pen flies across the page. I barely even realize I'm sitting in a public place.

Finally, the melody and lyrics release their grip on me and I'm able to put down my pen with a shaky hand.

I let out a deep sigh. All the rage, all the shame, all the disappointment I'd felt mere minutes ago in the photo shoot have now transmuted themselves into lyrics, filling me with a deep sense of calm and healing.

I wince. The photo shoot. Running out like that wasn't the best idea.

I go to fish my iPhone out of my purse's outside pocket and it almost slips through the hole in the stitching. I catch it before it smashes to the ground. Note to self—sew up hole.

I open the recording app and begin to hum the bits of the melody that have been floating around in my head, then softly sing the first verse and chorus to the tune.

Yes. I've recorded what I could've never found the guts to say out loud. To Eric, or to myself. But the truth is out now. And damn, it feels good. Because I've won. I've won because I didn't let my pain get the best of me. I've won because I'm the one in control of my own life.

Armed with this new sense of fresh possibilities

and limitless potential, I dump out the contents of my purse and start sorting through them, tossing the old receipts and gum wrappers into the trash nearby.

Ah yes, here it is. My fingers close around a crumpled business card. I look down at the page of lyrics again. And smile.

✧   ✧   ✧

AS THE CAB weaves its way in and out of traffic on the freeway the next morning, I swallow the final mouthful of my second to-go chai and look around.

Large warehouses and looming gray storage units pepper the land on either side of the highway and I begin to wonder if I've made a mistake.

I clutch my purse closer, the precious page of lyrics tucked safely inside.

No. I want to do this. I *have* to do this.

For myself.

The cab speeds onward, merging onto exit ramps and then back onto entry ramps, over underpasses and under overpasses until my head is spinning trying to take it all in and keep track of all of it.

All the while, I watch the meter climb. And climb.

Why is this place so far away from everywhere else?

I really hope it has a washroom because I drank way too much chai.

Finally, we pull onto a regular street. The cab slows down to avoid potholes as we drive through a residential area that looks like it's seen better days.

I swallow again. Wonder if I gave him the wrong address.

But no. I double-check the card again as the cab pulls into a gravel parking lot.

Thundercloud Music, 4656 89th Street West, Toronto.

It's the right place, all right.

I swallow again as I survey the collection of buildings, all looking like they were built by Communists somewhere back in 1984. Drab, gray concrete blocks and corrugated tin roofing. And there's a chain-link fence directly in front of me, topped with—I squint—barbed wire?

I thought this was supposed to be a recording studio, not a prison? And I thought McCloud was supposed to have money?

"Um, can you wait here for me?"

The cab driver waves a hand. "Sure, sure."

I hand him the fare and unbuckle my seatbelt, open the door and get out.

I crunch across the gravel toward the main building, wishing I wasn't still wearing my stilettos. A sprained ankle is the last thing I need.

I reach the door safely and look around. There's not a soul here. If it weren't for the silver Volvo that's parked nearby, I would really begin to worry.

I raise my hand to the door and knock.

Chapter Eight

"VICKY?"

Damn it. McCloud's not supposed to remember who I am.

He cocks his head and I realize he's waiting for a reply. "Um, hi." I offer up the only fast answer I can think of and, for extra measure, extend my hand.

McCloud's grip is warmer and firmer than I remembered, his fingers long and strong. And that relaxing effect...seeping...through....me....

I notice the corners of his eyes crinkle up as he smiles, his green eyes even greener than I remembered, as he stands there in his ripped jeans. That oh-so-soft-looking blue Taylor Guitars T-shirt.

My heart pounds.

Crap. Now I can't remember what I even... Oh yeah, the song.

McCloud releases my hand.

I blink. Clear my throat. Take a breath. Clear my head. "McCloud, I want to record a song I just wrote and—"

A male voice calls out, "Hey McCloud, so we're going to get that final mix in tomorrow for *Santa Baby*, right?" I hear footsteps coming down the hall.

The footsteps are getting closer even as I keep talking.

"You see, the song's about broken hearts, disillusionment and—" I snap my mouth shut.

Crap! (I *thought* that voice sounded familiar.)

It's Eric Black.

How can he just show up? Okay, so I'm the one who's "just shown up" but why does he have to barge in on this? Hmm, probably because he's recording a Christmas album.

"What's this about disillusionment?" he says, looking at McCloud and then me. "Oh, hi, Vicky. I'm sorry again about yesterday. I'd be happy to give you some comp tickets to a show to make up for it."

I dig my fingernails into my palms. Take a calming breath. That's really nice of him, actually. "Uh, thanks. And uh, hi."

Eric leans against the wall in his neatly pressed dress pants and crisp white button-down. Despite everything, I feel a tug of longing.

The hallway's long and narrow, the bare bulb flickers and I hear a man's voice, filled with enthusiasm, beside me. "They let me have it for a song. Now I can build the studio I've always wanted."

He gives my hand a squeeze and I look up at him, his face obscured by smoke from his cigarette. "That's wonderful, sweetheart."

A sense of yearning fills me. I blink, and the scene's gone. It's McCloud and Eric standing there. No one else. I shake my head, annoyed. And a little scared. Am I going crazy? Is this place haunted?

"Hey, if you need a backup singer for that song, Vicky, keep me in mind." Eric looks up from his texting. "Gotta mix it up a bit in between all these Christmas tunes." He grins.

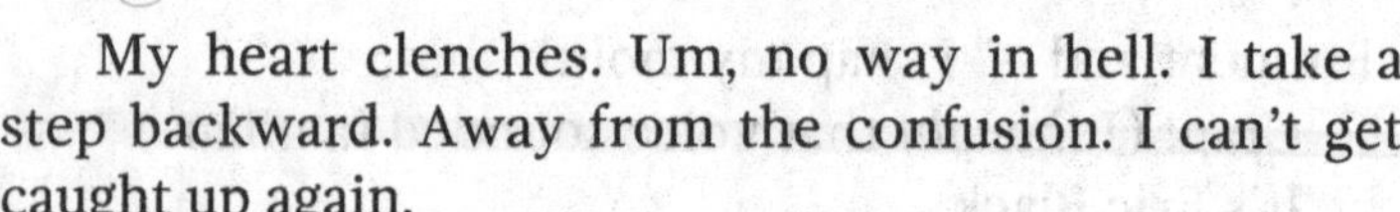

My heart clenches. Um, no way in hell. I take a step backward. Away from the confusion. I can't get caught up again.

McCloud glances over his shoulder at Eric, then back at me, his gaze questioning.

Time to make my escape from this nightmare. It was a ridiculous idea to come here.

So I spin around. Big mistake. All at once, that extra chai I drank in the taxi hits me and now I have to really go.

"Oh, um, do you have a washroom I can use?" I whisper to McCloud, as I dart a glance Eric's way. Fortunately he's now talking on his phone and isn't paying attention to us.

"Down the hall and to the left."

"Thanks." Hefting my purse over my shoulder, I keep my head up and make a beeline for it.

I shut and lock the door. Whew. What the hell was that? I look down and see my hands are shaking. So I close my eyes, lean against the door and force myself to take deep, cleansing breaths, trying to shove the anger away.

But it doesn't work. Argh. I could never work in the same room as Eric Black. I just might be tempted to strangle him.

I feel a sob building. I shove myself away from the door and head to the toilet.

After I'm done, I head to the sink and slap my purse down on the counter with more force than necessary.

Argh! This is all screwed up. I stare at my reflection. Scrub the brimming, angry tears away.

My purse slouches over. Grrrr. Even my purse has given up.

I lean down to snatch it up after drying my hands and march out of the bathroom, my chin held high. I make my way back down the hall toward the door.

McCloud is busy writing something down on a piece of paper. Eric's not in sight.

I open the door to leave but hear movement behind me.

"Vicky, wait a second." McCloud comes nearer and I take a step back.

He rubs the back of his neck with his hand. "You never finished telling me about this song of yours."

"Oh, um, there's nothing to say." I shift my weight. "I've changed my mind. And you're too busy, anyways, what with Eric's album." I give a nervous laugh and glance at my watch. "Oops. Gotta go. I have a flight to catch." (Such a lie. It doesn't leave for hours yet.) "Thanks anyway!"

McCloud looks like he's about to say something, but before he can, I turn and walk out the door, back to the waiting cab.

I get in. Shut the door with a sigh.

The cab pulls away. And as the babble of the radio and the hum of the tires lulls me, a deep sadness, followed by relief, washes through me. It's over. Thank God.

I think I need to just settle for a nice boring accountant or something.

✧ ✧ ✧

I WHEEL MY purple carry-on through the maze of people milling around outside the domestic departures terminal at Pearson International Airport. I grip the black plastic handle tighter as I make my way inside past the WestJet ticket counter. I feel more than a little smug as I notice its long line. Thank God I opted for online check-in. The fastest way to leave all this drama behind me.

Reaching security, my mind wanders as I scan the faces all around me in the long line. Of course, I check out the hot guys. That's what standing in long lines is for, you know. Except somehow, they all keep looking like Eric Black. I close my eyes for a brief moment, forcing myself to take a deep, cleansing breath.

That's over. It's *over*. He's not single, he's not interested and, what's worse, I think I still feel attracted to him.

Ugh. I wish I'd never come to Toronto.

On the bright side, though, the humiliation is over and hey, at least I racked up a few more frequent flier points. I just might get that free ticket to Hawaii.

I open my eyes. And now I'm seeing guys who look exactly like McCloud. Geez. My mind won't shut off, will it?

In fact, there's a guy who's wearing the same kind of Taylor Guitars T-shirt that McCloud had on... I sigh as the line moves forward and study my toes, hoping the guy's left my line of sight when I look back up.

But he's closer now. Much closer.

And I can see that he *really* looks like McCloud.

Oh no.

My throat seizes up.

It *is* McCloud. And he looks...panicked? Harried? What the heck is he doing here? Does he have a flight to catch?

I watch him more closely. Yeah. His eyes are darting around, and he's scanning the crowd, almost as if he's looking for someone.

Huh.

But whatever. Not my problem anymore.

I turn my attention back to the line. The security checkpoint's getting closer. Better get my e-ticket ready. So I reach into my purse for my iPhone.

But it's not there.

No big deal. I dig around. Maybe it's in the side pocket. I dig around some more. Nothing. My heart rate speeds up. I'm almost at the front of the security line. If I've somehow lost it—I check my watch—I don't have enough time to go back to the ticket counter to get them to print me another boarding pass.

Crap. Crap. Crap. *Angels, universe*, I plead in my head, *please help me.*

Wait. Maybe it's in my suitcase? When did I last have it? I kneel down on the polished tile floor, unzip my bag and begin sifting through the contents, anxiety buzzing through me.

The line flows around me.

What am I going to do if I can't find it? Oh God. I'll be trapped in Toronto forever.

I'm chewing on my lip and pawing through my underwear when I sense someone approaching from behind.

I look up.

It's McCloud.

Um. I hastily cram my pink lacy flamingo-patterned panties back into a corner, shut the suitcase lid and zip it up before standing.

McCloud's holding out something sparkly and

familiar-looking. "You forgot your phone."

"Thank God. I mean..." For some reason, I blush. "Thank you, McCloud."

"You're welcome. It was in the studio washroom. I tried to catch you, but you had already gone. So I rushed over here as soon as I could get away from the studio and searched all the ticket counters and the concourse. Couldn't find you. But then I found out that the next flight to Regina wasn't till five-thirty." He gave me a steady look. "So I waited around, and here you are."

He falls silent.

"Next!" The woman at the security checkpoint waves the person in front of me forward.

"Well, I need to go now." For some reason, I feel tears prickle. "Thank you again," I repeat, and then swallow the lump in my throat. "Goodbye."

The woman waves me forward.

McCloud falls in step beside me. "I have a confession to make."

That makes me pause. People move ahead of me.

McCloud shifts his weight. "I'm sorry, but I listened to your song on your iPhone."

"What? How?" I guess I can't be too indignant. I'm the one who wanted to share it with him in the first place, after all.

"The recording app was still open. Vicky, listen. I'm confident enough about the pieces of the song I heard that I want to produce it for you."

I sigh. Wasn't I done with all of this? I study him a second. Why is he showing so much interest in this? In me? Or am I just confusing art and life again? No. I can't do this again.

All those dashed expectations, all that hoping and wondering and praying and searching for signs. Reading way too much into every little thing. All the humiliation. Well, I'm sick of it. I'm tired of the drama I always end up creating for myself. I've had enough of that rollercoaster, and I want off.

"I can't," I say. "I just…can't."

I'm back at the head of the security line. My hand tightens on the handle of my suitcase. "Goodbye, McCloud."

Goodbye, fantasies and overblown expectations. And hello, reality. I'm done with crazy musicians.

The woman at the checkpoint gestures to me.

"Don't run away," I hear McCloud's voice behind me.

"All passengers on WestJet flight 4563 to Regina, please make your way through security."

"I'm not running. I'm walking away. In purple sandals, if you haven't noticed. Now if you'd just let me *do* that—"

"I really believe that it's a start to a good melody and lyrics."

"So produce it yourself. I'm tired of empty promises, all right?"

He tries again. "It's not an empty promise, Vicky. I think that—"

Good God. He's more persistent than a pit bull crossed with a piranha. "No." I shake my head again, glaring at him. "I think that this conversation is over."

I turn to the woman at the security checkpoint and hold out my phone for her to scan.

"It's the kind of stuff you have here that I've really been wanting to get back into, actually." McCloud says

it so softly I can barely hear him.

Yet something in his tone makes me look over my shoulder.

He ruffles his hair absently. "To be honest, I'm looking to shift away from the complicated, synthetic stuff." He shoves his hands in his pockets.

And then I feel my resistance softening. He's put himself out on a limb for me. Well, for my art, not *me*. But still.

"Final boarding call for WestJet flight 4563 to Regina."

A smile starts to form. It's kind of sweet, actually. He believes in me when no one else—not Sylvia, not Eric, not Jacques—really does anymore.

I feel respected. Honored. I feel...validated, because at least *someone* is paying attention.

Just like he did back at the Jeggs.

A swell of appreciation cuts through the last of my anger and resistance. And his green eyes. He really he does have beautiful green eyes... No. Stop. His eyes have nothing to do with this.

Besides, he isn't doing it for *me*. He's doing it for my art. And maybe that's the best gift ever.

"So the song would be kind of like one of Taylor Swift's?"

"Kind of like her early stuff, yeah. Just vocals and one or two instruments."

"WestJet is paging passenger Vicky Waverly."

I barely hear it. "Well...that might be kind of...fun."

The woman at security eyes me. "Make up your mind, lady. You're either going through security or you're not." She scowls.

I grin at her and take back my phone before she can scan it. Because, I realize suddenly, McCloud's right.

"WestJet is paging passenger Vicky Waverly. Vicky Waverly, please report to Gate D-25 for your flight."

Screw the flight. This is an opportunity to be a better woman. To rise above my circumstances—well, my anger and broken-heartedness, anyway—and I can't turn that down, now can I?

Chapter Nine

I PACE BACK and forth as if I could dodge between raindrops as I check my watch. Ten minutes till twelve. He said he'd be here. Of course, I'm ten minutes early.

I shove my glasses up the bridge of my nose. Not that it does any good, because the raindrops still splash the lenses.

The rain intensifies. I give up pacing.

Five minutes.

Where is he? Argh. Musicians. This was a dumb idea.

I start pacing again, but it's harder to walk because my frilly top and jeans are now sticking to me. And I sort of think I'm starting to smell like a wet dog. (When was the last time I actually washed these jeans?)

Then, abruptly, the rain stops. The sun comes out.

At that precise moment, McCloud appears. Ha, universe! Don't think I didn't pick up on that little bit of symbolism.

He's holding a black milk crate full of cords and has a set of keys in hand, his dark gray T-shirt sticking to him quite appealingly, and his dark hair starting to curl slightly from the damp.

"Sorry I'm running late."

"Actually, you're two minutes early." I grin.

"Still." He grimaces. "I hate to keep people waiting. I planned to be here at 11:30, but the launch I was at last night went super late." He gives me a sheepish, apologetic look. "Slept through my alarm." He shakes his head. "I'm getting too old for that stuff."

He jiggles the key in the lock. The door swings open. "You look drenched," he says, putting the carton on the empty reception desk. "I have some towels around somewhere."

I feel myself blushing. "Um, thanks but, uh, I'll be dry soon enough."

I follow McCloud into what must be a meeting room.

"Before we start, there's something I didn't mention." I twirl a strand of my hair around my finger. "I can't afford to pay you, um, much. Not anywhere near what you need for like, a high quality product. I got fired from my job and then blew almost all my savings coming here—meals, the hotel room, and that photo shoot for my now non-existent book. And Jacques the photographer's fee is nonrefundable."

"There doesn't need to be any huge expenses, really, because it doesn't have to be a high-quality recording. Just a demo track. You're not looking to put it up on iTunes or anything, right?"

"Uh, no."

"Well, then. It'd be maybe $300."

"But wouldn't it take, like, months or something?"

McCloud shrugs. "Doesn't have to take too long, really. Because you've done the hard work already—coming up with the lyrics and the bare bones of that melody. A few days to get the rest of the melody down; find the right instruments to use; record the vocals, then mix it."

"Oh. Okay."

"So, before we head into the actual pre-production and recording of the song, we need to get the lyrics straight, pick out the hook, stuff like that."

"Okay." The hook?

"Have a seat."

As he nods to the '50s-era furniture and we settle into two chairs, I slide my Mac out onto the table, unzipping its purple clamshell case.

"Nice touch." McCloud nods at my glittery guitar stickers surrounded by fake purple gemstones encrusted on the lid of the laptop. Okay, so maybe glitter stickers aren't professional or mature. But hell, the butterflies flitting around in my stomach probably aren't either.

I clear my throat. "I, um...well...I didn't think I was a songwriter, exactly." I fire up the laptop.

"You know, there's a quote I read somewhere that goes like this: 'give yourself permission to do it badly.' And hey, that's what producers are for. To help the artist achieve the big-picture creative vision and to sort of, at the risk of sounding cheesy," he laughs, "bring the song to life."

"Oh, I get it. Kind of like an editor would be for a novel."

"Bingo. So let's see the full version of what you have here."

"It's called *You Never Gave Me What I Wanted*." I angle the laptop toward him at the exact moment he leans toward me, peering at the screen. Our shoulders brush.

I stiffen and move subtly away.

McCloud acts like he doesn't notice. Just pulls out his own Mac and brings up ProTools and his email. "Why don't you send it to me, so I have a copy? It's mccloud@thundercloudmusic.com."

"Okay." I squelch the feeling of déjà vu while quickly copying and pasting the song into the body of an email and sending it to him.

He leans back in his chair, a look of studious concentration on his face, and I pretend not to notice the way his muscles flex as he crosses his arms across his chest, looking so—

No. Vicky. Do not go there. Too dangerous.

"Your hook, the theme of the song, is great—not getting what you want. And that catchy chorus—*you never gave me what I want, gave me what I want, gave me what I wanted*—works well as the title, too. I wouldn't say you're not a songwriter. It's just a different genre than novels, is all. Now, we just need to delete some of these verses. Oh and you need to tell me who it's about."

He looks at me, expectant.

Oh God, no. I stare at the screen of my laptop blankly, feeling the blush start to creep across my cheeks.

"Who is it about?" he asks again.

Argh. No way can I tell him who it's about.

"Who?" I blink at him, feeling like an owl, but none the wiser.

"Yeah. Who."

"Is this necessary?"

"Yes. It is. Because right now, the song's a bit confusing. You have all these verses but we need to hone in on which ones are the best to use. So we have to

answer five simple questions—who, what, when, where and why. Oh, and how."

"That's six."

"You got me there." He shifts back to serious, and back to the computer screen. "Need to get rid of the so-called writer's dilemma here."

I bristle. "Writer's dilemma? I'm a novelist. I know how to write." I'm not sure why I'm offended. Probably because the pain of my book failing is still so fresh.

"It means when you as the writer know who and what the song's about, but the listener doesn't."

"Oh." I relax. Right. Of course he wasn't personally insulting me.

"Answering those questions creates a clear foundation for the song. The plotline, basically. So who's it about?"

"Okay, okay. It's about a guy."

"A guy. No name?"

"No." I stare him down, daring him to force me to spill my secret.

"All right." He blinks and breaks eye contact, then makes a note on his laptop. "Now about the where, why, when and how."

I twine my fingers in my lap. "Well, the when and where is, uh, when this um, guy..." I trail off. Should I tell him? Suddenly I really, really want to. I feel strength and a certain courage fill me as McCloud sits there, expectant, fingers poised over his laptop. "When I found out he was married. After I had sort of, well, given my heart to him when I first met him. Although it was clearly an illusion on my part."

McCloud just nods. "Makes sense. Okay. So we can

delete these two middle verses you have, since they're repeating what you already said in the beginning." He taps a pen on the desk. Guess this is just all in a day's work for him.

Somehow, that makes me feel better, not worse. Less personal. "And the how, well, was in person." I delete the verses he's talking about, then cross my arms across my chest as a barrier to the anger I still feel toward Eric. Hmmm. I re-read the lyrics again. They do make more sense now. McCloud knows what he's talking about. I feel a tiny *ting*! of happiness.

"And the why was because I'd gotten my hopes up after he sent me email and Facebook messages." I sigh. Not that our correspondence *meant* anything to him, though. *That* delusion was all in my head.

"Great—then these other verses can stay. This is great."

McCloud grins and suddenly swivels in his chair, grabs the guitar that's on a low stand beside him and settles the instrument on his lap. "Building on that base you came up with..." There's a thoughtful look on his face.

He strums a few chords. "This could be the start of the chorus." I hear the excitement in his tone.

My foot begins to tap along with the beat he's creating.

As his fingers move, I notice for the first time the carved obsidian ring on the middle finger of his right hand and the silver filigree one on the pinky of his left hand. I frown. Does that mean he's married? Or is it like a promise ring or some sort of engagement ring? Not that I've ever heard of a male engagement ring... But I'm not assuming anything anymore.

McCloud continues with his earlier train of thought. "The song's sort of like a diary entry meets a knife in the back. What do you think?"

The obsidian one's not on his ring finger. Is that some sort of scroll design? Oh wait. Maybe it's a snake? Hmmmm. Or...Oh, right. He asked me something.

I feel the first fluttering of artistic excitement build within me. He's totally asking my input. He wants to know what I think. "I like it. And I like the way you think."

Oops. That came out way flirtier than I'd intended. Gak. What is it with me?

"Good. That'll make things easier for the collaboration." He puts the guitar back on its stand.

Right. Of course. What was I even thinking? He's being professional. And I'm being ridiculous. I give myself a mental shake and try again. "That sounds good. It's sort of sweet and angsty at the same time. Revenge of the good girl." Which is totally how I'm feeling.

That phrase sets off a chain reaction in my imagination, and suddenly I'm creeping down a back alley at night, wearing an all-black skintight cat suit, a ski mask pulled over my face while—

"Hey, that'd be a great title for an album, actually. *Revenge of the Good Girl*. Or *Good Girl's Revenge*." McCloud makes a few keystrokes, then turns back to me. "Now, about the vocals. You sing?"

"Um." I blink, pulling myself with a bit of effort back to the present moment and McCloud's question. "Sorry, what?"

"Do you sing?"

"God, no. I sound like a strangled cat."

McCloud doesn't reply, just does some clicking and scrolling on the computer before he swivels it to face me.

"One word. Auto-Tune."

"Technically, that's two words."

"Well, if you want to get technical..." He winks. "It's hyphenated."

"So you're just gonna doctor up my voice? Listen, my forte is writing lyrics and stories. I have no intention of becoming a singer, okay?"

"You won't. It's not for an actual track," he says, patiently. "This is just the demo. The whole point is to get big artists to take a look at your song to see if any of them might want to cut it for their own records."

"But people are gonna think that my voice really sounds good." What is he doing now, trying to manipulate me and my art? No. No. Vicky. Don't go there. That's ridiculous. It's just a song, not my heart.

I must be radiating tension or suspicion, or both, because McCloud exhales and rakes a hand through his hair. "Listen, how about we just—" He clears his throat. "How about I just listen to you sing the song and then go from there. Sound fair?"

"All right. But don't say I didn't warn you." I add, "Even though I did take voice lessons last year." I babble on. "Maybe that's why that song came to me? Anyway, those lessons were just beginner lessons and I don't really know what I was thinking because the concert I did afterward, a friend recorded it and I just...ugh. It was pretty awful. Even though it was the first time I'd ever used a microphone and ever sang in front of an audience before, the memory of how bad I sounded is permanently burned into my brain..." I trail off, somewhat bewildered at my verbosity.

McCloud just nods. "We'll add a bit of reverb to the recording mic, which will add a bit of dimension to your voice and then make sure the melody's in the right key for you, too. Might take a little tweaking to find the right key." He pauses.

I bite my lip. "Oh, if that's too complex... I mean, if it's simpler to do it a different way, I can..."

"Oh, I like a challenge."

My heart pounds a little faster.

"Don't worry about that." He stands up. "Then, if we need to, Auto-Tune can take care of anything else."

Hastily, I stand too, not comfortable with his 6' 3" frame towering over me. "What about accompaniment?"

"I thought I would do it, on the guitar." He nods toward the one on its stand.

Suddenly I feel lightheaded. "Oh."

"Let's head over to the isolation booth and do a take with vocals only. Just to get the big picture." He checks his watch. "I can squeeze that in before my first appointment of the day. Then we can go back and fine-tune the lyrics side of things tomorrow if we need to, while we're working on the melody."

Uh. I feel my palms start to sweat. God no. I can't do this. I can't sing in front of him. What will he think of me? He'll judge me. Laugh at me.

Get a grip on yourself, Vicky. Breathe. You're the one who asked for this. You can do this. It's not like you're performing at the Jeggs or anything. Just keep calm. You can do this.

I follow McCloud down the hallway. He opens a door to the messiest room I've ever seen. It's a lot larger than I thought it would be, and smells like stale donuts.

On one wall is an almost floor-to-ceiling window that looks out into the room with all the sound equipment.

Carpet lines not only the floor but also the three other walls and the ceiling, and there's a big black microphone affixed to a shiny chrome stand in the center of the room. But that's where the logic of it all ends.

Cords and wires trail all over the place; empty plastic milk crates and folding chairs are stacked against one of the walls. Random pillows are strewn on an old red couch, and there's a birdcage and a white screen hanging from the wall opposite me.

I have to squelch the urge to start tidying up. "Uhhh, I thought isolation booths were smaller."

"They usually are. This place also doubles as a film and TV production studio; I have a friend in that biz, so things tend to get mixed together."

He flashes a grin, then gestures to the mic. "All yours. I'll be on the other side of the wall there."

I nod. He makes a move for the door; I start to feel panic build, and babble again. "But I haven't warmed up!" All the while looking over my shoulder and not watching where I'm stepping.

I trip headlong over the bunch of cords on the floor.

Lightning quick, McCloud places a hand on my arm to steady me. Now he's near enough to me I can smell that Ivory soap. I swallow and shake off the

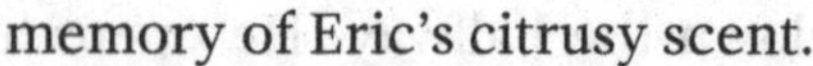

memory of Eric's citrusy scent.

"I think that if you sound a little off-key, it gives your voice a bit more character. Just do a few warm-ups and then go into the song." The warmth of his hand seeps across my skin for an instant. He drops his hand, turns and shuts the door behind him.

I wait and watch as I see him enter the room on the other side of the glass and sit down at his Mac. He puts on his headphones, takes a seat on the red leather swivel stool and starts pressing buttons and sliding sliders up and down.

"Whenever you're ready."

I nod. "Okay. I'm ready." No I'm not. What if Eric Black comes in?

Hmm. It feels weird to hear McCloud's disembodied voice around me.

I smile. It's kind of like a friendly ghost or something. Who cares if Eric comes in? He doesn't know who I'm talking about, anyway.

That's my little secret.

That thought allows me to relax. Okay, okay, I can do this. I close my eyes and take a deep, cleansing breath. In. Out. In. Out. I swallow once, twice. Inhale one more time and then say a silent prayer to the creative forces.

All at once, I feel it. I hear it flowing through me. I cock my head and open my mouth, just letting the words flow out from me without any thought, without any focus except to listen, really listen.

The emotions build within me as I think, once again, about Eric and how I felt like he wasted all my time, led me on a wild goose chase with all his pretty words... Accurate or not, I don't care, I'm just mad at him.

As I sing the words, softly at first, a flood of emotion rises within me. I feel that anger and angst rise up as if awakening from a deep slumber. I relax even more, and it's almost as if I'm not singing—it's more like the words are coursing through me, and I am the channel, the outlet for the emotion and feeling embedded within them.

All those times that I trusted what he said to me, trusted his view and trusted what I thought were real promises, real words that would have some weight, that would be made good on. But no. My eyes narrow and I spit out the next lines.

I see McCloud's toes tapping along and his head starts to bob. He whips out a pencil and begins drumming on the side of the table, slapping his free hand down against the metal.

Feeling vindicated and validated, I keep singing. Louder. And stronger.

Because whatever. *Whatever*, that little voice in my head screams. Eric just doesn't get it. Doesn't get me or any of this or what I'm feeling. All at once, as the lines flow through me, I can feel parts of my heart loosen. It's like the words are a balm to my soul. Cliché, I know. But true. Too true. The anger swirls through me, healing me in the very act of being expressed.

I see McCloud begin humming along.

And suddenly I forget. I just let go of everything but the music. About everything but this moment in time where I'm being real. Pouring forth my true authenticity and my heartache.

I get to the second verse. By the time I'm about to start the chorus again, I see the start of a smile spread across McCloud's lips until there's a broad grin sitting there.

I feel an even bigger surge of joy as I just keep going. This is my art. My moment. My reality.

That's when I catch McCloud's eye.

And freeze.

I close my mouth with a snap and a blush flames up my cheeks. All of a sudden I feel naked. Oh my God. He's watching me. Listening to me. Hearing my art. Seeing me at my most vulnerable. I was showing him my real self. I force the vulnerabilities away as I finish the third verse. God, this is awesome! I feel a surge of joy shoot through me. Making art kicks ass! I sing the chorus again.

> *Cuz you never*
> *Gave me what I want*
> *Gave me what I want*
> *Gave me what I wanted!*

And one last time:

> *You never gave me what I want*
> *Gave me what I want*
> *Gave me what I wanted...*

Before I realize what I'm doing, I jump up from my chair, my body humming with all that joy swirling through me, supercharging me and making me feel like I can do anything—maybe even fly! I put my hands on my hips and then get up on top of the chair, standing there, balancing on the hard plastic before stepping up onto the table, an almost orgasmic pleasure shooting through me.

I told him! I told him off and now I have the last word and this is so awesome because now I can do whatever I want and say whatever I want and he never even has to read it or hear about it or anything else. I'm free!

I open my mouth and sing the chorus again, a sense of completion and satisfaction pulsing through me.

I stop and look around. It's only then that I realize I'm standing on top of the table, my hands on my hips, a smile of triumph on my face.

Sheepish, I hop down off the table and waltz into the production room.

"Feeling better?"

I laugh and plop down into the cushy leather chair next to his. "I've been reborn!" I fling my arms into the air.

McCloud turns and looks me straight in the eye, a spark of something in his gaze.

I hastily sit up.

"Yeah, that's a kick-ass melody. I think we can totally work with that. Definitely a place to start. And I love that one burning emails line." He chuckles. "Remind me to never ignore Facebook messages from you."

I feel warm as I see his eyes move from my face momentarily down to my best Prada knock-off blouse. I'm suddenly glad I wore my flamingo-print lacy push-up bra. With matching panties.

"Well, you're batting a thousand so far."

I flip a lock of hair out of my eyes and sit up a little straighter.

As I do, a shadowed look crosses his face and the

playful moment fades, his professional mask falling back in place as if it never left.

McCloud clears his throat. Stands. "Right. I have to go. Got my next musician showing up. But we'll get started on putting down the melody tomorrow, now that I've heard how you sing the whole thing. Meet me here at 8:00 a.m."

✦ ✦ ✦

GRAY CLOUDS, BLOATED and ugly, hang over the city this morning. Looks like it could get nasty out. But it's a beautiful day in my heart. (Plus, I got a discount when I extended my hotel stay.)

I feel like McCloud has a really good understanding of my artistic vision. I've thought about it since yesterday; it's totally fine that he's drawing the whole professional line. In fact, that's what I told him I wanted, so he's listening, which is a good thing.

I step across the threshold, holding a steaming chai in one hand, my laptop in the other. "Good morning, McCloud," I call in the general direction of his office as I push open the door of the studio my usual 10 minutes early.

No reply.

Chapter Ten

H E'S NOT IN his office. Hmmm. Or in the conference room. I crane my neck. Not in the isolation booth, either.

I continue down the hall to the production room. Peer in the window. But the lights aren't even on.

Yet I can see a silhouette in the dim light filtering in through the window. It's McCloud.

All alone. With just his guitar for company.

I catch my breath.

His eyes are closed, his brow furrowed, his whole posture tense. Angry. But his fingers are producing the most amazing melody. I listen, transfixed.

Pain seems to radiate through him, through the guitar, through the notes themselves. It sounds like a raging thunderstorm.

He sways slightly, and then his mouth opens, and snatches of my lyrics come out. In such a raw and helpless swirl of rage, sadness and longing that it steals my breath.

I keep still, wanting this moment to go on forever, feeling myself drawn into the space he's created, that space of vulnerable reality that he's unknowingly sharing with me; a space of compassion and allure. Because what I'm seeing isn't any illusion—it's truth.

And I realize I want that.

To be there for him. With him. I want to help him

as much as he's helped me.

Shame suddenly fills me. I shouldn't be watching this. Or him. I can't. It's too private. Too...intimate.

But still I stare. He's given himself over to the melody; his head falls back and I can see the strong line of his throat and shoulders in the early morning light. Words, accompanied by the melody that's now changed key and tone into one of sad, almost-stifled restraint, leave his lips. "...wants the fantasy...wants the fantasy...wants the fantasy..." The minor chord builds and builds and his lips part, his chest rising and falling with each word as his fingers let the notes ring out; the anguish in his tone builds even as the music crescendos into crashing silence.

I hastily back away from the door. Check my watch. Chew my lip. It's now one minute to 8:00.

Time to show up on time. I retreat back down the hallway and then spin around. Take a deep breath. Okay, I'm going in. This time, I march purposefully down the hallway and rap loudly on the door.

A moment later, I see the lights flick on and the door opens.

"Vicky." His eyes dart away, then back to my face. For a flicker of an instant, I see a trace of vulnerability lingering in his eyes. He blinks, rakes a hand through his hair; his guitar still slung over his shoulder.

He clears his throat.

My heart does a funny little hitch and I find myself blurting out, "Oh, so this is where you've been hiding."

He swiftly rearranges his expression. "Yep." His lips rise into a half-smile. "And you're early."

"Yeah. Sorry about that." I twist a stray curl

around my finger. "I have that tendency. Must be the writer in me." I laugh weakly at my failed joke.

I feel my tension ease as I see that he's now fully recovered his composure. "Well," he says, "come in." He even smiles.

There's an awkward silence. I walk over to the table and put my laptop down.

McCloud smoothes down his slightly wrinkled shirt, then moves to his laptop. He brings up Pro-Tools. "Gotta record everything, even these early drafts, so we have something to go on when we master the track."

The bench squeaks slightly as he takes a seat at the keyboard and settles the guitar onto his lap. "Okay, so I'm thinking that bit of the chorus we worked on yesterday? G major for it, with maybe E minor for some of that moodiness. Some angst." He plays a few chords. "I thought we'd focus on getting down the rest of the chorus, to start."

"Okay." I sink into a folding chair as he continues to strum.

"Yeah."

My foot starts moving to the beat. "I was thinking about what you played yesterday. Maybe it needs to be a little faster. With a bit more..." I squint at the ceiling. "Emphasis on the downbeat."

He changes pace and tempo. "Like this? What do you think?"

I look into his beautiful green eyes. And I want to cry. My song. He's playing my song...

All at once, there's a flash of *something* within me, a fleeting residual tug of sound and light and sadness. In those seconds, in that echo of feeling, it's like a hidden part of myself is holding onto something I know I should've long since forgotten. I wish, for a confusing, shameful instant, that McCloud could *be* Eric.

What? No. I can't think that. More importantly, *why* am I thinking that when I know Eric is off limits? Annoyed at myself, I shove the residue of thought away and start to hum the chorus.

McCloud joins in with my vocals. I hear that same rawness I witnessed earlier. But he doesn't flinch or cringe away. He just sings.

"Yeah. Yeah. I like this." I feel a frisson of excitement as I join him with the chorus. My heart keeps time.

"Good, good," he murmurs, concentrating on playing the chorus. He repeats it a few times, nodding in time to the notes he's creating.

"So I know you heard the melody I had for this. I want you to hum the melody you had in your head, what you sang yesterday. Except without the words. Just la-la-la."

I give him a deer-in-the-headlights look.

He leans back. "Just la-la-la. You can do it. Your vocals need to be layered in on top of my guitar. All together. Kind of like making lasagna."

"Lasagna." I nod. "Okay." I take a breath. "Okay." And then I burst out laughing. "Sorry, sorry. It seems so silly. Like I'm in kindergarten."

"Kindergarten's a valuable grade." He grins. "It's okay. Just try again."

I nod. Hold my breath. Let it out. "Okay. Laaa-laaa-laaa lalalala, lalalala, lalala LA-LA!"

"Good." He brings the guitar back to his lap.

"Good." He plays what he hears me hum. "Yeah. Yeah. I like this." He echoes my words. Unconsciously?

As he keeps playing, I feel the energy building. The energy of the song. The energy of our collaboration.

I feel a surge of joy. Wow. I'm really doing this. This is—I feel a shiver—exactly what I *wanted*. And McCloud looks like he's enjoying it as much as I am. This is exactly what Eric didn't give me...*couldn't* give me, I realize sadly.

But McCloud is. Freely. Openly.

My heart flutters. Am I just jumping to conclusions again? Even if he is, he's probably just enjoying the creative process. Not my company.

We continue fiddling around with the basic melody, adding on, taking away notes, for what seems like hours, but is probably only twenty minutes. It's starting to sound pretty good. Like a real song.

I feel another jolt of happiness. I'm having so much fun; I forget all about Eric in the face of this playful sharing. "Oh! What about putting in a little piano for embellishment?"

McCloud stops strumming. He sets the guitar down on a nearby chair and glances at me. "Since we've got the chorus down, yeah. I like that idea." There's a pause in which I hear the pounding of my heart. (Or is that just the sound of the rain drumming on the roof?) "Join me?"

I sit down gingerly on the bench next to him. When he moves over to accommodate me, the shifting of his weight reverberates through the bench and into me. I will myself to breathe normally. Professional, Vicky. Professional.

"What about the rest of the lyrics?"

"We'll add them in a minute."

He strikes a chord on an upper octave with his right hand, layering a brittle, staccato melody overtop it with his left hand. "Something like this?"

He turns to me and I place my left hand just above the keyboard, fingers hovering. I can smell cinnamon. His gum? Argh. *Vicky. Focus.* I clear my throat. "That sounds perfect. Do you ever make a mistake?"

He winces. "Oh, I'm far from perfect." But he keeps playing.

I tear my eyes away from his nimble fingers and lick my lips before gnawing on the bottom one.

He does a few more runs, head cocked, his expression thoughtful. Then he stops.

"Here. Try out a few variations yourself. It's your song, after all."

"But I don't know how to play piano. I'm not—"

"I'll show you." He reaches across the keyboard and places his left hand gingerly on top of mine.

Gently, our fingers descend together onto the smooth white keys. And for that moment, all I know is the warmth of his hand.

"This major chord should harmonize with—" He takes his hand off mine and picks up the guitar. "—the chorus."

He's right. "Let's try a few of the verses with that."

So we do.

"That sounds totally awesome. And then maybe we could do something like this..." I trail my fingers down the keyboard, allowing my hands to guide me, gaining certainty even as I let myself dive into the mood, the tone, to the lower register. "Because the song has sort of a darker feel to it, too, you know. She's not happy with him at all. There's—" I frown, remembering, as anger flashes hot through me. "—a lot of pent-up rage there, too. He's just broken her heart. Destroyed her illusions." I bring my hands down on the low notes like I'm some sort of phantom pianist caught in the eye of an inner maelstrom.

"Or we could do this." His eyes are questioning me again. His fingers move back from the guitar to the keyboard, firmly issuing another chord. I'm suddenly warm.

"No. Too Baroque." I laugh at the sudden vision that pops into my head. "I can just see Bach or maybe Beethoven banging away on some harpsichord in a cathedral, white hair all wild and eyes crazed."

"Oh, you mean like this?" He brings both hands down onto the keyboard with full force. The atonal, almost asymmetrical quality of the notes that jump out leave my ears ringing. I shake my head, mouthing no at him.

He just mock-leers at me, pulls a crazy face and continues his melodramatic playing.

"Whoa. That's pretty creepy." I laugh at his expression. "Especially with the added effect of the rain on the roof." I raise my eyes to the ceiling. "Have you ever thought about acting?"

"Well, actually I've done an audition or two."

"Aren't you Mr. Modest? I knew it." I give him a playful shove. It feels so good to feel this comfortable.

He stops playing abruptly, reaches for the guitar and scoots away from me.

Crap. Did I do something wrong?

He picks up the chorus line again on the guitar. I

tell myself I must be imagining any standoffishness. I watch as he moves his fingers a few half-steps back up the scale. The tendons and veins visible just under the skin on the back of his hand move delicately, almost gracefully. I find myself transfixed by his long, lean fingers. So strong. So sure. I feel my pulse quicken.

"But there are these lighter notes, too." McCloud's right hand reaches for the top end of the keyboard. "Maybe these notes could signify her heart shattering, but also represent hope, in a way. Because she is, after all, still a romantic at heart." He plays a few more notes without looking at me. "And maybe, maybe at the heart of it all, she still," his eyes slide to mine, "wants to believe in something real?"

I meet his gaze. He looks back at me, his eyes holding something deeper and warmer than anything I'd ever noticed before. "Exactly," I whisper.

"Hey, man."

I turn and look at who's interrupting. Might have known.

"So you're almost done with this little demo track?" Farley strides over to us. "We need to start on my album. I have so many things I need to be doing."

I want to stab him in the eye with a fork. I curl my hands in my lap instead.

"We'll get there," McCloud answers without looking up. "Just chill."

Farley nods and shoves his hands into the pockets of his low-rise jeans. "Right," he says, his tone casual, easy. McCloud doesn't see the annoyance flit across Farley's face.

But I do.

"Vicky, there's something McCloud failed to mention to you."

Before I can say anything, he adds, "Didn't he tell you?" Farley acts as if he's talking about the weather. He's carefully avoiding McCloud's inquisitive look. Farley continues. "You mean McCloud here didn't mention how he always comes in second place with the ladies?" Farley sidles up to the keyboard. I feel like I might puke.

Mortified for McCloud, I glance over at him. His fingers are frozen in mid-air above the guitar strings.

Farley smirks. "Surprised, Vicky? Well, nice guys finish last. It's the frontmen women want. Sure, McCloud gets to work with you, but he—"

"Farley, can it. When you get stressed, you get stupid—we'll get to your project soon enough. All right?" He fixes Farley with a steely glance. Farley mutters something under his breath and scuffs the toe of his shoe on the floor.

McCloud stands abruptly. "That's good for now, Vicky. Let's meet back here tomorrow afternoon to run through things one more time so we can put all the elements together."

He doesn't answer the unasked question in my gaze.

Chapter Eleven

"SINCE WE MADE lots of progress yesterday, we're all set to record the final version of the guitar, piano and vocals, mix them together and then lay down the track today." McCloud takes a seat beside me and sets his open laptop next to the soundboard in the production room.

I feel self-conscious with my rain-frizzed hair, slightly damp shorts and sockless feet inside my brand-new Keds.

McCloud pulls up ProTools as if nothing at all happened yesterday. And who knows. Maybe it didn't. Besides, McCloud's personal life is his personal life. None of my business.

"Before we start with your vocals, I'm going to go grab a coffee. Want anything?"

"Oh, um, sure. If there's any tea, that'd be great."

"I think there might be some Red Rose around. Not sure how old it is... Could be expired. None of us really drink tea here, so you might be taking your chances."

"I'll walk on the edge."

He chuckles. "Okay, I'll be back in a sec."

He leaves. I tap my fingers, mentally adding the lyrics to the melody running through my head. Hmmm. I think it'll work, it sounds pretty good, in fact. I glance at McCloud's screen. Beside ProTools, I see that he has Google Chrome up displaying a website. FACTOR. What does that stand for?

I giggle to myself as my imagination zooms into overdrive. Maybe it's some sort of secret spy organization and McCloud's actually running the front for it.

I pull up the same site on my own laptop and study the webpage. Nope. It looks like some sort of music industry thing—and oh, look, here are next year's Jegg nominees. I start scrolling through the list, noticing there's a video beside each one.

Eric Black's been nominated.

I feel a stab in my solar plexus. Do I really want to torture myself and read this? I thought I was over it. Him.

But you know what they say about curiosity and cats... My fingers hover over the play button.

Wait. This is perfect. It's like a test. If I'm really over him, then I can totally watch this video without emotion.

I click play, hold my breath and turn the volume down really low—what would McCloud think if he actually discovered me doing this?

Eric's rich vocals come through the speakers, his suit immaculate, his hair perfectly styled. So different from McCloud.

My heart jumps as I watch Eric's handsome face. I sigh. Get a grip, Vicky.

The camera zooms in as he turns to the woman beside him on stage. He extends his hand to her and they move to center stage together, singing together.

No. I can't look. Can't listen.

It's too late. I'm transfixed.

All at once, images tumble through my consciousness, superimposing themselves in my mind's eye until they're all around me.

My best silk dress. The third date. I feel the sweet, firm warmth of a man's embrace as he gently presses me against him. We twirl around the dance floor. The singer, plaintive and heartfelt, makes the ballad fill my heart with longing. Yearning. Burning.

Cigarette smoke hangs hazy in the air, the heat and crush of dancers all around us almost overwhelming. I lay my head on his shoulder. It feels so right. So right.

Though his face is shadowed by the brim of his fedora, I can feel the way he's looking at me with deep, warm regard, his lips curving up into a smile...

Just as quickly, the images vanish and I'm staring at the laptop again. My breath comes in gasps as I come back to myself. I blink rapidly and it takes me a second to remember where I am—in this cold, metallic chair, with a leaden weight on my heart; this strange mixture of sorrow and joy.

My heart squeezes. The video's still playing. Eric takes the female singer's hand and twirls her as the music swells...

Why can't that be me, why can't it? Not him and her.

I shake my head, knowing I'm being utterly ridiculous, even as I feel tears prickle, the remnants of longing and yearning pulsing through me, even as I hungrily drink in that joyful, soulful look in his eyes.

I can't watch this, yet I can't seem to stop.

As the final notes fade, I watch through a haze of tears. He'll never look at me like that, will he? He's not mine. He never will be.

My nose is running. I snuffle the back of my hand against my face. I wish that McCloud had some tissues around here—

"It's really pouring out there now."

I freeze.

"Heard some wicked thunder when I was in the kitchen. The good news is the expiration date on this was only from—" He stops talking when he sees me. He puts down the drinks and comes over.

"Vicky? You okay? You look—"

I cover my face in my hands. "Don't say it. Like the bride of Frankenstein. Part two. In 3-D."

As if on cue, the lights flicker. "Very funny, universe," I mutter at the ceiling.

McCloud calmly sits down by me. "I've seen worse."

"You have?" I sniff again while scooting away from him.

He hands me a Kleenex. "Three sisters. Two older, one younger. What's wrong?"

Heat rises to my cheeks. "It's silly, really." I feel a surge of anger at myself. "We need to get back to the song. You don't have time for this."

"You sure? Confession's good for the soul. I used to be Catholic, I should know."

"Oh, it's nothing..." I hastily shut the lid of my Mac. "Just some visions that might mean I'm going insane." I laugh. "While I was watching this silly duet that I got a little too emotional about." I start shredding the tissue McCloud gave me.

His eyes light with enthusiasm. "Visions? Cool. You could make some kick-ass music video with fodder like that...and from all that angst you're emanating, this might be useful energy to put into another song."

I shake my head vehemently and scrub the Kleenex across my cheeks, removing the last traces of my tears. "I was just...just *such* an *idiot*. I can't believe I was dumb enough to let myself get that carried away by all of it. Again. All of..." I gesture to my head, "the *illusions* inside my own head." I laugh. "And then to actually *cry* about it. Cerise is right. I've been living in fantasyland far too long."

God, it feels good to talk to someone who's actually listening.

"I-I'm sorry." I start to get up. "I've been totally unprofessional; it's pathetic and weak; and I think I need some fresh air before we get back to work."

"Maybe it is pathetic and weak. But sometimes you just need to be pathetic and weak in order to find your strength."

"You're like a denim-clad Obi-Wan, you know that?"

He holds up his hands. "Don't go making me into some sort of intergalactic saint. Although *Star Wars* is one of my favorite movies. Vicky, there's..." He reaches out a hand toward my face. "Don't move."

I stiffen as he leans closer. Is he putting the moves on me? No. I try to shrink away.

His fingers are almost close enough to brush my cheek.

Surely he's not...

That's when the power goes out.

❖ ❖ ❖

IT'S PITCH BLACK. McCloud swears. "Guess that thunderstorm did its damage."

I open my laptop back up. Now there's an eerie whitish glow all around us.

"Sorry. Just a piece of Kleenex stuck to your cheek." He plucks it off with deft fingers.

"Oh." I feel a surge of mortification mixed with disappointment. I thought... "Um, thanks."

McCloud gets up and gets out his iPhone.

"Out in this neighborhood, it could be hours before it comes back on again. The warehouse district isn't exactly high priority for power outages. But downtown is fine, according to Channel 9."

"So what does that mean?"

"It means we need to finish this today. Next week is crazy for me. I'm signing three new artists, have some launch parties to go to, plus there are a few performances I'm doing backup vocals for. And with Eric's wrap party this weekend, and you spending more time here than you thought, well, I think we'll be burning the midnight oil. I have some sound equipment and a guitar and keyboard back at my place."

I bite my lip. "Umm, okay." I follow McCloud out the door of the studio. I look around, curious about what his car will look like.

But there's no car. Or truck.

It's a motorcycle.

❖   ❖   ❖

"BEEN ON A bike before?" He hands me a spare helmet and then gets on.

Um. We're going to ride a motorcycle in the rain? "Once." I hated it. And I fell off.

"Good. Then you know the drill." He turns the key in the ignition and the motor settles into a throaty purr.

I put on the helmet and tighten the chinstrap and then get on behind him. There are so many reasons why this is a bad idea.

For instance, where should I put my hands? Ack. I really wish there was some sort of motorcycle etiquette. Such as, if bike passenger is not a girlfriend, place hands on shoulders. But if bike passenger *is* a girlfriend, wrap arms around waist.

Those green eyes slide to mine in the small circular side mirror and my heart pounds. There are no such rules.

"Ready?"

No.

I swallow and nod, determined not to let him see me wuss out. "As I'll ever be."

"I'm going to be moving pretty fast to keep up with traffic, so you're gonna want to stick close and keep a firm grip around me."

I scoot forward and my inner thighs now press against his. I lick my dry lips. (God. Now would so not be the time to remember that I've always had a thing for men's thighs.)

With my hands on his shoulder, I can feel them rise and fall with his steady, even breaths. I shiver and wish I could scoot further away so I wouldn't have to feel my chest squished against the long muscular planes of his back. He's too... I bite my lip. Male. Virile. Tingles surge through me. He's too warm, too solid, too real. I pray the ride's short. (Whoa. Gotta stop thinking in double entendres.)

He revs the engine and I'm forced to cling to him as he pulls out of the parking lot, into the street and onto the *freeway*.

Everything is moving at warp speed. I'm gripping him so tightly that I wonder if he's going to pass out.

Then he actually speeds up again.

I can feel my fingernails digging into my palms.

I hunch down, using McCloud as a shield, and squeeze my eyes closed. Steady, Vicky, steady.

Suddenly, I feel his weight shift to the left as we sink into a curve at like, 800 miles per hour.

I pry one eyelid open.

Oh God. I'm going to die.

I pop my other eye open.

I feel so alive. So awake right now in this moment.

The laughter bursts from my lips and suddenly I'm giddy. Because, my God, this is...this is...pure freedom!

All this air and storm and the world around me. The wind whips my hair around my face.

I love this! I love it. I see the beauty now. Everywhere.

In the pieces of highway litter, in the muddy semi-trucks, in my helmet hair and McCloud's ripped jeans. Even in the bugs.

It's this great big circle of harmonious, connected oneness. Motorcycle riding is my new religion.

McCloud slows down. Signals. He's changing lanes again.

Oh. I guess we're almost there? Damn it.

He pulls into a reserved parking spot, cuts the

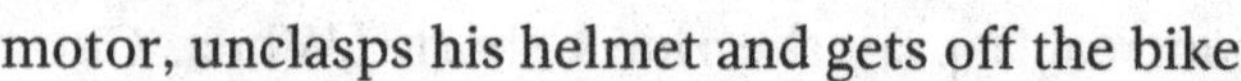

motor, unclasps his helmet and gets off the bike.

I get off the bike too, still feeling a tingle of nirvana.

It's gone by the time McCloud turns and locks the helmets in the saddlebags and meets my gaze again. "Okay there? Let's go inside."

Inside, it turns out, is a shiny steel and chrome condo complex that looks like—I crane my head back—somewhere Donald Trump would live if he were Canadian.

By rights I should be fingernail-bitingly nervous as I step onto the elevator with McCloud.

After all, he's still an almost-stranger. And I'm going up to his place—on the top floor. Yet I feel like he's trustworthy.

I follow as he walks down the hallway to a door at the end and fishes for a key in his wallet. I hear the snick of the bolt being turned. "Come on in."

What if I'm wrong? What if McCloud's actually an axe murderer? I chew my lip as he opens the door and I follow him across the threshold.

Or worse, a vampire? It does seem kind of dark in here. (Note to self—lay off those vampire romance novels.) My man-meter is more than a little skewed, thanks to my ex, Jason.

I fumble with untying my tennis shoes and shrugging off my damp denim jacket.

"You okay?" McCloud helps me out of the jacket and puts a hand on my shoulder for a second. A sense of ease returns. I'm fine, I'm fine. Of course he's not my ex. I take a breath. Right. It's just McCloud.

I swallow. Nod. "Where should I put my jacket?"

"Oh, here. I can take it." He hangs it up in the hall

closet before taking off his leather jacket and boots. He looks strangely cute in his sock feet.

I glance at the shiny purple polish on my bare toes and feel vulnerable. "Thanks."

We move into the living room. Floor-to-ceiling windows line the far wall, letting in the gray watery daylight. But somehow, from this bird's-eye view, what should be a drab and dull cloudbank bursts into infinite shades of silver, charcoal, obsidian, steel and ash instead.

"Beautiful." (Ah, the state of motorbike Zen has returned.)

"Wicked," he agrees. "Especially when it storms like this. You can see the sheet lightning for miles." He grins as he stands by the window. "I love heights."

I see his reflection in the glass. Notice a small smudge of something—dirt? oil?—on his cheek, and the way his thick, wavy black hair is still in disarray from his helmet, with strands sticking up completely out of order.

I sigh. He looks perfect. Of course those emerald-green eyes and that sexy stubble starting to darken his strong jawline don't hurt, either.

He turns his head. We're looking into each other's eyes.

Without thinking about it, I reach out and quickly brush the dirt from his cheek, his stubble prickling my fingers. "Gotta pay you back for that Kleenex favor."

Instead of the smile I'd hoped to see, a shadow of sadness flits across the surface of those green eyes.

I feel my throat start to close up. Has he been hurt too? Compassion fills me, for his humanness. For his vulnerability.

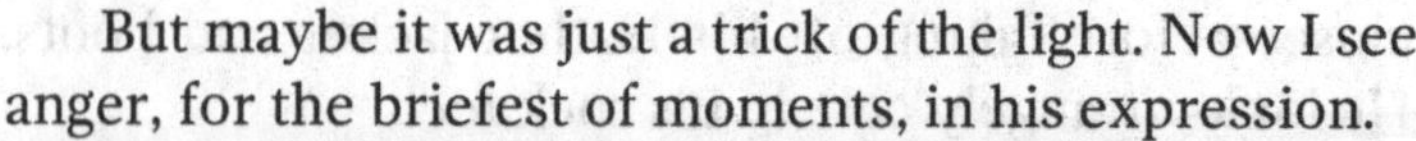

But maybe it was just a trick of the light. Now I see anger, for the briefest of moments, in his expression.

He clears his throat and turns away. "I'll go grab the guitar."

I frown. "No," I say, watching the rain stream down the windowpane. I reach for the silver doorknob embedded in the panel of glass and wrench it open. I want a do-over. I want to erase all the pain and sorrow and hurt and fears from his expression. And from my own. I want to really feel alive—fearless. I want him to feel better.

Before he can escape, I grab his hand and pull him with me out onto the balcony, the rain pouring down on both of us. I raise my face to the wind and cold and laugh, feeling the raindrops on my tongue.

He looks like he just stepped out of a Taylor Swift song: all soulful eyes and sinful good looks. Somehow, that emboldens me.

I reach out to touch McCloud's face, my fingertips tingling as I bite my lip. Why did I ever hold myself back before? The gray-blue light filters across his face and I see my hand as if it belongs to someone else. That's what fear does to you. Yet those are *my* fingers that are about to touch his skin, just the way I wanted to touch him back in March. Just the way I've dreamed about with Eric. Just the way Jason mocked me for—No. McCloud's not Jason. He's not. He's not going to make fun of me or slap my hand away and then mess with my head.

His skin, though cool from the rain-damp air, burns through me like fire. I swallow, powerless to the fear rising within me. I swallow again and beat the fear back. No. I'm being ridiculous.

McCloud's jaw tightens. I see the storm brewing in his eyes and I know I shouldn't do this to him. I snatch my hand away. "Sorry. Um, this is awkward. Now we're both all wet."

"Yes." His gaze is level. "We certainly are."

A bolt of lightning spears the sky.

"S-sorry. Let's just um, go back, uh, inside..." I spin around and narrowly avoid banging into the glass door.

"Careful there," he murmurs, way too close to my ear. I dart past him. I can't escape the loud silence hanging between us now as I drip water onto his gleaming floor.

He hands me a towel.

"Well, let's get started, then." I switch to the safety of professional mode, feeling disappointed when he does, too.

"We'll go over it a few times." He sits down on the white leather couch and pulls out his guitar. "I know this isn't probably how you expected or envisioned the final recording of your song to be."

I laugh nervously. "If I've learned anything in the last few crazy days, it's how expectations just trip you up."

"Don't I know it. I'll take this back to the studio when the power comes back on over there, mix and master it. Then you can come by and pick up a hard copy before your flight leaves Monday." I catch a look of wistfulness on his face as he looks at the guitar. "This was my grandpa's. Gave it to me as my birthday gift the day before he died." He runs a finger along the guitar's curves. The pale varnished wood gleams.

"Oh." I don't know what else to say.

He plugs in a few wires from the guitar to his lap-top, then picks the guitar back up.

"So. You ready?" He looks at me, all business now, except for a few strands of that wavy hair that have fallen across his forehead.

How could Farley have said McCloud comes in second with the ladies? I feel a surge of compassion, which gives me the courage to relax my guard as I take a seat on the matching leather chair beside the couch.

He strums the intro chords.

❖   ❖   ❖

How many more times will we have to go over the final cut? I dutifully open my mouth and start to sing the first verse. For the seventh time.

I'm so tired, so maybe I'm just overreacting and underappreciating. The final notes fade away at last.

"I think it sounds really good." McCloud nods in satisfaction.

"I like how both the vocals and the guitar are gon-na be on one track now, instead of two separate ones. I like it better without the piano, too. Is that okay?"

"Sure. I'm the producer," McCloud says. "But you're the artist. If you like it better without the piano, then we'll leave it without the piano."

He puts the acoustic guitar down. Gives it a pat. "Nothing like 1950s quality. And music."

"I disagree. The 1940s are the best—jazz music like Eric Black's."

"Au contraire." There's a glint in McCloud's eyes. "Wait here."

I watch him walk across the room and go up to the loft. I notice a bookcase in the corner by the stairs. It's stacked to overflowing.

Ooooh. I have to go check out his shelves. My heart beats a little faster as I examine it. A beat-up copy of *Guitar for Dummies* is side by side with a memoir of The Beatles, stacked on top of an autobiography of Paul Anka, which is next to several Kurt Vonnegut novels, a bunch of Green Lantern comics and *The Great Gatsby*.

McCloud comes back down the stairs, iPod dock in hand.

"You weren't kidding when you said you had respect for writers."

He locks eyes with me. "I admire people who have ways with words." He holds up the iPod. "Case in point: Buddy Holly." McCloud holds out his iPod and motions to the couch.

"Who?"

"Says the vintage fangirl? You don't know the man who practically invented rock 'n' roll?" He raises an eyebrow and turns on the device.

"Hey, I'm not the expert like *some* people in the room."

"We'll fix that." He grabs his ear buds, stuffing one in his ear and handing me the other one.

"Now just listen." McCloud grins. "This is *Every Day*."

At first I just sit. Then I catch my toe tapping along. And now I'm humming. "This is so much better than Elvis."

"You have excellent taste." He leans back against the couch, looking thoughtful. "Did you know that

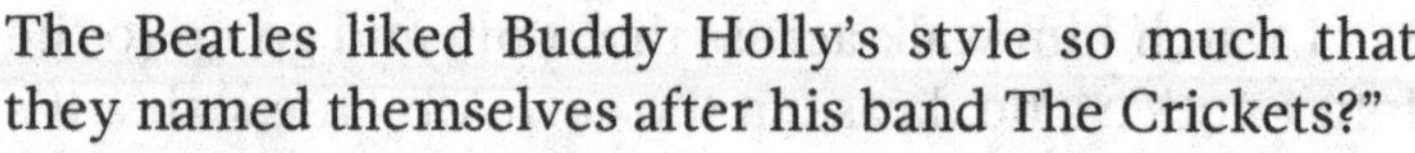

The Beatles liked Buddy Holly's style so much that they named themselves after his band The Crickets?"

"Really?"

He nods. "That's what Paul Anka said. I read his autobiography a few months ago. Those guys—they were legends in the making." He looks at me, but there's a faraway expression in his eyes. "They just made music. They just did what they truly loved. Had that passion and heart."

"Like you," I whisper.

He ducks his head, picks up the guitar again. "No. I'm a fraud. I've just followed in their footsteps, not blazed my own trail. They were at the center of something cutting edge. Revolutionary..."

There's such longing in his voice that it takes my breath away.

"Taking chances. Making music their own. They left an indelible mark on society, on culture, on the entire face of music as the world knew it." His eyes are bright. "To be that great, to be your very best..." He plucks the strings. "Is what music really means to me."

McCloud runs a finger along the body of the guitar with reverence. I shiver.

"That's what it's all about, really. What's at the true heart of rock 'n' roll. What I think that some people in the business have forgotten in the face of fame and the glare of the spotlight."

His lips thin and I see his jaw clench. "Crazy musicians or no, sometimes there's no excuse for bad behavior." He shakes his head almost imperceptibly.

Chapter Twelve

H E PUTS THE guitar away. Closes the laptop. "Well, I think that's a wrap."

My stomach growls. Loudly. I put a hand on my abdomen and laugh self-consciously. "Good. I could use a wrap. I'm hungry." I stand up. "I should go. It's way past time for me to get something to eat."

McCloud glances at his watch. "It's almost 7:30." He pauses. "Listen, you don't have to leave. I mean, unless you want to. That is, uh..." He rubs the back of his neck in a gesture I've come to recognize as a nervous one, before meeting my gaze. "Would you like something to eat before you go? I can make something. Burgers sound good?"

"That's fine. I'll help."

"Great. I'll thaw out the panties—" He freezes mid-step. "P-patties. I meant to say *patties*."

I snort. I can't help it, the image of lacy underwear encased in icicles flashes through my mind. "I'm glad," I say between giggles, "that I'm not the only one who makes Freudian slips now and then."

❖ ❖ ❖

MCCLOUD GETS A box of patties out of the freezer. "You can slice this, if you like," He says, handing me a tomato. "Knives are in the second drawer on the left."

He pops the patties in the microwave, then moves to a cabinet underneath the far counter.

I rattle through the contents of the cutlery drawer, trying to dislodge the giddiness that's suddenly crept up on me. I pick out a knife, grab a nearby cutting board and concentrate on getting the tomato slices exactly even.

"Ouch!" I drop the knife with a clatter. So much for concentration.

"You okay?"

I inspect my finger, sheepish. "Yep. The knife only nicked the first layer of skin. No blood."

I go back to slicing. But my eyes stray from my task when he bends over to get out a countertop grill. Though the label on his jeans says Gucci, I wouldn't care if he bought them from Wal-Mart because they serve their purpose—making him look hot as hell.

It's tragic, really, if Farley is to be believed. McCloud certainly deserves more than a consolation prize with women. The way his soft cotton T-shirt stretches so nicely over the hard muscles of his chest, the way his fingers press the meat as he transfers the patties from plate to grill top...

I hear the sizzle of meat and swallow. Burgers are so not what is making my mouth water right now. I eye his biceps. "Okay, this is gonna sound like such a line, I know."

"What is? I might like a line or two." He grins.

"You'll think I'm crazy."

"Too late." But there's warmth in his tone.

"Do you work out?"

He glances at me, a mischievous look in his eyes. "You're right—that is a line. But the answer is no."

"Oh."

"Stage crew. Those speakers are heavy."

"I didn't think someone who'd won four Jeggs and got a Grammy nod would be hauling around speakers." Oops, now he knows I stalked his profile online.

"Can't beat a free workout. Besides, winning Jeggs shouldn't change who you are," he says. "Still need to pitch in."

"That's what Tay does too. Er, Taylor Swift, I mean. Not workouts with speakers," I add hastily. "What I mean is, she stays grounded and all that."

He studies me for a second. "You're a big fan of hers, aren't you?"

"Now *that's* an understatement. She's my... I really admire her. She's accomplished so much..." I sigh. "I want to inspire as many people with my own art as she has with hers. I know everyone says that, but I'm serious. And," I laugh. "I'd love to bake cupcakes with her, too."

"Speaking from personal experience, anything's possible when you're committed to your dreams."

Eric's face flashes through my mind. "Yeah," I mutter. "Look how far that got me."

McCloud stays silent.

"I know, I know. I was waxing poetic about Taylor Swift, but the truth is, I'm really pissed off right now. My whole book plan flopped and—I don't mean to complain, but I feel so helpless. And I don't know what to do about it." I raise my chin. "But I'm going to just forget about all that for now because I'm starving."

"Good. The burgers are ready."

I help McCloud set the table and then we sit down to eat.

"You know, not to go all Obi-Wan on you again, but maybe that all happened for a reason." He takes a bite of his burger.

"Maybe." I take a bite too.

The silence is deafening. I push my tomato around on my plate with my fork, as if I might find the answers written there—about Eric and his wife. I know, I know. I need to get over it. I really, *really* want to. But somehow, I feel compelled to ask. *Have* to ask. Asking is the way I'm going to get over this.

"So...how long have you known Eric?" I fiddle with my fork. Why am I doing this to myself?

McCloud gives me a speculative look as he takes a sip of water. "Since he started out. Five or so years."

"How did he meet Zosia?"

McCloud shrugs. "On tour in Latvia. Latvians love jazz."

"So she's Latvian?"

"Yes."

"She works in town?"

"At the Bay, in the jewelry department."

"And has he..." I see a flicker of annoyance or maybe frustration in his eyes.

"Go on. Ask whatever you like."

"Has he always sung jazz?"

"Yes." He crumples up his napkin.

I'm about to open my mouth to ask something else when McCloud speaks.

"Is this what you came here to do, Vicky? *Really?* Come on. I thought you were smarter than that. Sure, you have your crazy moments..." He runs a hand through his hair. "But going on and on about Eric..." He shoves his chair back and stands up, starts picking up the plates and putting them in the sink. "It's not healthy." He turns on the water and dumps in detergent without looking.

I feel sick. "That's not what..." But I know he's right. That just makes me madder. "Who are you to talk? Freud or something?"

"I thought you liked my advice."

"You barely know me."

"Are you sure about that?"

"What the hell is that supposed to mean?"

"I don't know. You're the New Age chick. Why don't you figure it out?"

"You know what I think? I think you're just jealous."

"Jealous? Of what? Some sort of crazy fangirl obsession?"

"Hey! I thought you were the nice guy here."

"Even nice guys have their limits. Damn it, Vicky, that's the problem. Can't you see—"

"I see the sink's overflowing." I cross my arms.

"Crap." He turns off the tap.

I clear my throat. "Um, can I help you do the dishes?"

"Wash or dry?"

"Dry."

He hands me a dish towel; I take it from him and our hands brush.

But I don't dare do anything about it.

We stand at the stainless steel sink in silence, the only sounds the clink of dishes and the splash of water. Once or twice, our hands brush again.

A sense of peace sneaks through my defenses. I find myself letting out a contended sigh and a smile

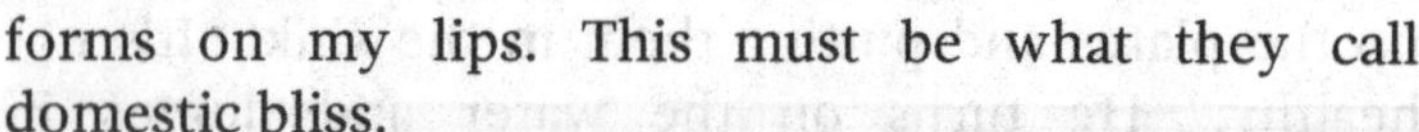

forms on my lips. This must be what they call domestic bliss.

"Bored?" McCloud washes the final dish and hands it to me.

"Oh, no. That was..." I blush. "A sigh of peace, actually."

McCloud pulls the plug in the sink and the water starts gurgling down, making a loud sucking noise as the last of the suds and dirty dishwater make their exit.

I start giggling. "S-sorry," I stammer. "It's just—" I gesture to the sink. "I don't know."

"Don't apologize for being yourself." He dries his hands.

I lick my lips. Why does he seem so good at actually *seeing* me? And why does that bug me so much?

He shifts his weight ever so slightly toward me.

I take a step back. Big mistake. I've trapped myself in a corner formed by the side of the fridge and the counter. "Why are you so perceptive?"

"Three sisters, remember?" His gaze doesn't leave my face. "Vicky," he says softly as he moves nearer, "I'm sorry about earlier. What I meant to say was..."

His hand, still hot and damp from the dishwater, makes me go cold as it comes to rest on the small of my back.

As his arm slides around my waist to pull me closer, I can't breathe. But not in a good way.

You don't deserve this, a tiny voice whispers inside my head. *You don't deserve to have a real man, a real relationship, a real anything.*

McCloud's lips descend to mine.

It's much safer that way, don't you see? the nasty

voice in my head continues, its seductive purr louder than the soft, warm slide of McCloud's lips against mine.

The only thing you're good for is clinging to illusions. Fantasyland's where you belong, it snarls. You're a writer, after all, and writers always live in their heads— and that's where your love life has to stay, too.

McCloud is not Eric. I feel a burning, choking sensation in the back of my throat. McCloud isn't just an iconic ideal to cling to. My fingers dig into the butter-soft folds of his shirt.

I let out a whimper. There's no denying it now. McCloud is *real*. His kiss deepens. And he's interested. Why was I pretending all along that he wasn't?

The muscles of his chest move underneath my hands as he pulls me closer still. Oh God.

Because it's safer to retreat. McCloud actually being interested in me means any sort of actual relationship would bring out my fears into the light of day. No. No.

I shove myself away from him and wince at the clear intensity of his green eyes now clouded with confusion. I can't take the heat. So I'm getting out of the kitchen.

✦ ✦ ✦

"DID I HURT you? Are you okay? What's wrong?"

I feel a wet trail of tears sting my eyes and glance up at him but say nothing.

"You don't think I'm scared as hell too, Vicky?" His voice is husky and he reaches out to me.

I don't reply or move.

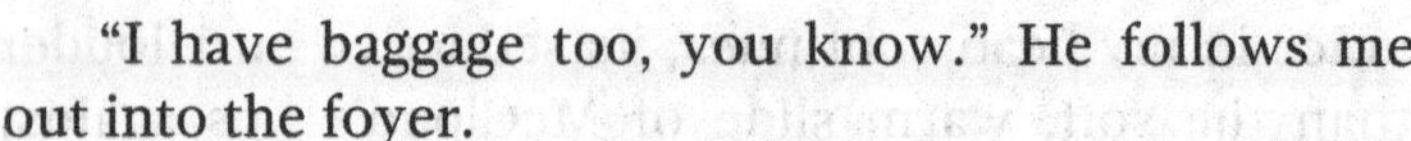

"I have baggage too, you know." He follows me out into the foyer.

I press my lips together and curse myself for wearing tennis shoes as my fingers fumble with the laces. (Hard to make a classy escape in runners.)

He shoves his hands into his pockets. "I'm divorced."

I look back up at him. My eyes widen.

"Vicky?"

I sloppily tie my other shoe and sniff.

"Vicky, please say something." He crosses his arms. "And please don't look at me like I have three heads."

"Well, you have at least two," I finally snap.

He says nothing. Just raises a brow.

I fake a coughing fit. "Um, um, excuse me. I need to leave." I stand up and fumble for the doorknob.

"I am a man, you know."

"Yeah, let's not go there, okay?"

"Where?"

"You know."

"No, I actually don't."

"Fine. Fine. You want the truth?" I shake my head. "You can't handle the truth."

"Why does that line sound familiar?"

"Because I stole it from a movie. But it's appropriate right now."

"And what if I might want to be somewhat inappropriate?" He takes a step nearer.

"D-don't you dare use your masculinity to intimidate me, mister."

"Why not?"

"God. You sound like a pompous jerk right now."

"Good. Because at least you're not running away."

I start to turn the knob. "That's my cue."

"Vicky. Just tell me what's wrong."

"Me. You. This. *Everything*."

"Why?"

"Because."

"Because why?"

"Because you're asking too many questions. Why do you even care?"

"Why are you getting mad?"

"Because you're putting your nose where it doesn't belong."

"Maybe I want it to belong."

"Your nose?"

He lets out a growl. "You know what I mean."

"We live in different provinces. I'm leaving Monday. You're not my type. And besides all that, we barely know each other."

"Those are all excuses."

"Legitimate ones."

"Why are you coming up with all these reasons for it not to work?"

"Why *aren't* you?"

"Because I'm a man. My brain can't multitask."

I open the door. "There's a thousand reasons why it shouldn't work."

"But only one reason why it should."

He goes to close the gap between us but I slip through the doorway. Why am I constantly running away?

Because I'm scared that I'll just collapse under the weight of all of this reality. And be crushed.

Even as I slam the door in his face, the realization

I've been hiding from slams into me—I'm *so* attracted to him. And that's *so* dangerous. Because love equals death, love equals pain. Love equals shame and fear and doubt.

My mind goes back to Eric. Zosia. And my ex.

Love is danger. Love is fear. Love is worry. Love is doubt. Love is not beautiful, kind, gracious or anything else. Love is a lie. Fear is the only thing that's real. And illusion is the only place to be safe.

Chapter Thirteen

I CAN'T JUST throw myself into his arms. Can I? But maybe that's the best way to get over myself and these silly fears.

I stifle a yawn as I approach the studio door; too many intense dreams last night about me, McCloud, tangled sheets, and cold showers.

I had to take one before I got here, in fact. I shift my weight as I eye the door. Force myself to breathe normally.

Maybe wearing this mini skirt is a bit much? After all, all I'm doing is picking up the finished track. Well, that and reclaiming my dignity. Okay and maybe trying to impress McCloud, too. Then I have to leave. I set my jaw.

Screw leaving. Screw staying. I need to be in the moment. So I heave open the heavy door. I need to do this. Be strong. Tell him the truth. I need to prove to myself that I can be the heroine of my own life. Never mind that I somehow have to put this huge mess behind me in a few days so I can find three jobs to pay off this huge debt I've amassed.

But it's not McCloud on the other side of the door.

It's Zosia.

She waves. I wince.

"Oooh, are your feet hurting? Those look like new shoes."

Crap. "No." I hastily cover my grimace with a grin as I step into the lobby. "I'm looking for McCloud, actually." I tug at my skirt.

"Oh, the boys are in some sort of meeting." She gestures to the shut conference room door. "With some...what do you call it? Bigwigs. Could be days before they're ever out. Cute skirt, by the way."

I tug on it again. "Thanks."

McCloud never mentioned a meeting. But why would he mention that to me?

She puts a hand on my arm and her flowery perfume drifts past my nose. "How *are* you?"

"Confused. McCloud said he was going to master a track for me today. I'm leaving tomorrow. I don't know..."

"Oh!" She snaps her fingers. "You leave that to me. Just come to our pool party tonight. Those boys could be in there for the rest of the day. I wouldn't want them to waste your precious time. Go out. See this beautiful city. And then come tonight." She winks. "McCloud will be there."

She rushes on as she sees my expression. "It's the wrap party for Eric's Christmas album." She links her arm through mine and smiles, her teeth dazzling, her hoop earrings jangling as she tucks a strand of her platinum hair behind her ear. "I know you're not supposed to have a wrap party for a CD, but my Eric, he's worked so hard on this, and well, I love any excuse for a party. It was my idea." Her big blue eyes fill with excitement. "Please say you'll come."

Hmmm. It would be the perfect opportunity to explain myself to McCloud. I could pick up the finished demo track, too. And maybe, just maybe,

Zosia does like me. She wants to be friends. But she's Eric Black's *wife*.

"To be honest," she continues in that Slavic accent, "I don't know many other Canadian women." She ducks her head almost shyly.

It'd be nice to make a new friend. Even if she is *his* wife. "All right." I give her another smile—a genuine one this time. "I'll come."

"Oh good." She gives me a quick air kiss on both cheeks. "I would pick you up myself, but I never learned to drive. So Eric, he will be glad to pick you up. You must not refuse. He'll be happy to help."

Chapter Fourteen

I STAND OUTSIDE my hotel with a sinking feeling that has nothing to do with the weight of my full bag as I shift it from one shoulder to the other.

God. I should've called a cab. Taken the bus. Why did I let Zosia talk me into the party invite? Into Eric picking me up?

It's too late now. I spot his silver Volvo pull up to the curb. I feel like I might puke. Nevertheless, I step up to the car, open the door, and get in. At least the scent of the leather interior is reassuring.

"Hey!" Eric says as I slide into the passenger seat.

"Hi," I reply, forcing myself to be cordial.

He pulls out into traffic as I fold my hands tightly in my lap.

"So what have you been up to?" His tone is bright; friendly.

It's a lie, I realize. He doesn't care about what I've been up to. I'm not special. At least, not to him. Why did I trick myself into thinking I was?

"Oh, not too much." I feel shyness take hold. "Re-reading Jane Austen, actually. My favorite book—*Persuasion*."

"That's right," he says. "You're a writer."

I look over at him. Despite everything, my heart opens up just a little at this tiny sliver of attention. Stupid heart. Why, oh why?

"Yep. I love writing."

"Not that I know who Jane Austen is, exactly. Would it be awful if I admit that I don't read much?"

"Nope," I lie. "Not awful."

Tragic. How could I have even thought that Eric and I were alike? That we were a perfect match for each other?

The bookcase in McCloud's apartment comes to mind. I can see the look in his green eyes, hear his words—*I have a lot of respect for writers.*

Does he still? My heart lurches.

I glance over at Eric. Stupid obsession. He pushes up his aviator sunglasses; merges onto the freeway.

"So, uh, thanks for doing this." I wish I could swallow the despair I'm feeling, wish he would turn the radio up a bit more to cover this awkward silence.

He gives me a grin. "No problem. My wife's always farming me out to do stuff for people. It's one of the things I love about her." He chuckles.

Love. Oh God. Love. All at once, I feel a strange sort of helplessness overwhelm me, and with it, the thought, *he's supposed to be mine.* I grind my teeth. Go away, useless thought. Go away. He's not mine. He never will be.

My hands clench into fists and I force myself to take deep breaths through my nose. It's way too hot in here, that's all. I press the window button and the glass slides seamlessly down.

I stare at nothing, trying to keep as far away from Eric as possible. But the Volvo is too small, and the only sound is the shifting of gears as he works the manual transmission.

Gears. Shifting.

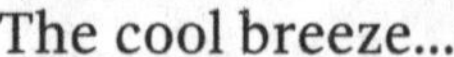

The cool breeze...

Out in the open air, the open highway, a man, his face shadowed by the brim of his fedora, is behind the wheel. A cool breeze is on my face. He's steering the Chrysler with one hand, his other arm is draped across the back of the seat. We're laughing.

Sunlight streams through the windshield.

I'm so happy. Ever so happy. Because we're going for a picnic out in the country. And I baked his favorite— apple turnovers, for dessert. He's humming—

"...song's a classic. You have great taste."

The images shatter as quickly as they came. Dazed, I frown and look over at Eric. "Excuse me?"

"That song you were just humming. I said it's a classic."

"Humming?" I blush under his gaze despite my best intentions. "I wasn't humming."

He gives me a funny look. "Sure you were. Just now."

I laugh and lie. "Oh, yeah, yeah. Must have been stuck in my head or something."

"I've always loved that one, you know. Always meant to record it; somehow never got around to it. Maybe on the next album."

I say nothing. But my eyes fill with tears.

The car slows. He downshifts, takes an exit off the freeway into a suburban neighborhood, then pulls into the driveway of a two-story brick house shaded by trees. "Home, sweet home." He turns off the engine and sets the brake. "Come on in." He opens his door. "My wife'll be out back, probably, and I've gotta go fire up the grill."

He hops out.

I open my door with a shaky hand and haul myself out, dragging my bag with me as I shut the door behind me, wishing I could so easily shut the door on whatever that was.

◆　◆　◆

"VICKY!" ZOSIA COMES over, all tan skin and perfect body in her red polka-dot bikini. "I'm so glad you made it."

I can do this. Be nice to Zosia. Avoid Eric. Find McCloud.

"Yep, I did. Um, I need to change into my swimsuit."

"Of course." She gestures, bracelets jangling. "The washroom is just down the hall and to the left."

After I change, I tie a wrap securely around my waist, then head downstairs to Eric's walkout basement.

All this will soon be over, I tell myself. I just need to pick up my copy of *You Never Gave Me What I Wanted* from McCloud, and then catch my flight home tomorrow.

Zosia introduces me to a few people. I'm not really paying attention. Where is McCloud?

I scan the crowd of people chatting away in their bathing suits and Santa hats while holding martinis. More people are out splashing in the pool. I can hear the sound of Eric's *Chestnuts Roasting on an Open Fire* through the open sliding doors.

"If you want, go get a drink." Zosia nods to the wet bar in a far corner. "Then you come find me and I'll give you a tour of the rest of the house."

"Sure." I nod, preoccupied.

I see McCloud at last, behind the bar. God, he looks sexy pouring himself a drink. I feel a tiny twinge of disappointment: he's not shirtless.

He glances up and our eyes meet.

That momentary inattention costs him. The drink he's pouring begins to overflow. He hastily mops it up with the bar towel that's tossed over his shoulder.

A bead of sweat trickles down my back. How can I face him? Tell him the truth? I chew the inside of my cheek.

Too bad I don't drink. And too bad the line's like, twenty-five people long. Oh well, I'll just head out to the pool for a little while until it gets less busy.

Outside, I perch on the end of a chaise lounge tucked into a far corner, bathed in the late afternoon sun. Maybe I shouldn't have chickened out and waited in line instead. But I couldn't exactly tell him the deepest secrets of my soul in front of Eric's guests.

I stifle a huge yawn and slip on my sunglasses and floppy hat. I scoot up the chaise and lean back. I really wish I'd gotten more sleep last night. Mmm, that sun feels nice. Maybe I could just stretch out here for a second? Rest my eyes for a minute...

✦ ✦ ✦

I BLINK AWAKE, yawn and stretch. That's weird. I don't hear... I cock my head. No music. And—I shiver—it's gotten kind of cool. And dark. It's just me and the guttered-out tiki torches.

I swing my legs to the side of the chaise and stand

up. Surely I haven't slept that long? What if McCloud's left?

Wait, I do hear something. I move toward the low murmur of voices coming from the walkout basement. The sliding door's still partly open, and light spills from it.

I peer in.

Eric touches Zosia's face softly, running a thumb down her cheek and smiling softly at her as she says, "We have another cause for celebration."

If I were the paparazzi, this would be an opportune time. I can't tear my eyes away from them, though I know I shouldn't be spying.

I hear him whisper, "Oh, honey, is it?"

Her eyes are shiny with tears. She rests her forehead against his as she nods. "We'll name her after your sister."

"Darling." Now his voice grows husky. He brings a hand to rest gently, briefly, on her stomach, then pulls her to him and kisses her lips.

I bite my lip so hard I taste blood. Oh God. Now would not be the time for a house tour, would it?

I whirl away into the semi-darkness, march around the corner of the house, and smack into the back of someone. A someone who is muscular and solidly male.

I leap backward. McCloud's the last person I want to see at this second. But God, what a sight. Because he's finally shirtless...

The purple twilight only serves to highlight every toned curve and smooth-muscled sinew of his back. I sigh. I'd caused him so much pain and discomfort. I'd run from this beautiful man. I feel tears threatening.

He'd been so beautiful toward me, but I'd thrown that all away and now I would probably never get it back.

Over the top of his left shoulder blade, the fading light brings into sharp contrast the blue-black ink of a tree tattoo. Leaves and branches drape across both broad shoulders before merging into a sturdy trunk around the middle of his back. It's the faint whitish scar that slashes the trunk of the tree in half as if it had been split by lightning that catches my eye. A wave of sadness seeps through me even as my fingers long to trace that scar, to find out where it came from and why, and if I can somehow do anything to make it better. The sadness only grows even as I see the roots travelling around the two irresistible dimples in his lower back before the ink finally disappears below the waist of his swim trunks.

He spins around. My fingers twitch as I see his dark dusting of chest hair.

"Vicky. I was looking for you. I have your demo. Zosia said you'd be out by the pool. I was just gonna go grab my towel—thought I might take a swim."

I jump in before I lose my nerve. "I owe you an explanation and apology about yesterday."

"So do I." McCloud studies the ground.

"The thing is..." I shiver.

McCloud steers me over to a chaise and drapes a discarded towel around my shoulders. I smile gratefully at him. He sits down next to me.

"My ex-boyfriend was..." I feel like I might throw up. "Abusive." I wrap my arms around myself, suddenly cold, even through the thick terry cloth. "One evening he pinned me down on his couch." My teeth start to chatter. "So I couldn't get up. And then he put his hand over my mouth and..." I can't continue.

"Oh God. I'm so sorry, Vicky," McCloud whispers.

It seems like the most natural thing in the world to lean against him and relax into his warmth. But I hold myself upright. "I went through counseling. Did the whole forgiveness thing. Sage-burning, New Moon ceremonies, intention setting. The whole shebang. I thought I was healed."

I dig my fingernails into my palms. "That was four years ago. I haven't really dated since and I...tend to run away from stuff." I hunch forward, feeling smaller and smaller.

I glance over at McCloud and see the hesitation in his eyes as he asks, "Do you want a hug?"

"Yes," I whisper.

He wraps his arms around me. Moments pass in silence. Crickets chirp. There's the low rumble of cars passing. The sound of our breathing.

I relax even more. "Zosia and Eric are going to have a baby." Whoa. That's not what I intended to tell him. I cross my arms and wish I wasn't half-naked right now.

He tenses and shifts away from me. I look up into those beautiful sea-green eyes, but they're suddenly devoid of warmth.

"No, Vicky." He stands. "You don't get to keep doing this."

I tense. "What?"

"Shutting me out." He starts pacing. "Bringing up Eric every time I try to get close to you. Why? Is it because I'm not *perfect*?" He spits the word out like it's poison.

"No. I'm stupid and ridiculous and hopeless. But I can't seem to let it go. Can't you get that?"

"The only thing I've been getting is nothing." He jams a hand through his hair. "I've been kind. I've been patient. I've listened to everything you had to say through this whole songwriting process. Damn it, I've enjoyed it. Enjoyed being with you, too. But you know what?" His jaw clenches. "I finally figured it out."

I jump up, my feet slipping slightly in the puddle I'm standing in near the pool's edge. "No. Don't say it. I *wanted* to collaborate, okay? I wanted to—"

"Use me as a substitute for Eric, didn't you? Didn't you?" He takes a step toward me. "Yeah, Vicky, I figured it *all* out. I know the song's about Eric. This whole goddamn charade was about *Eric*. And I was stupid enough to think—"

I don't dare move. Because he's right. *He's right.*

"Goddamn it." He slams his fist onto the teak table beside the chaise.

I flinch.

"Fuck. That hurts." He shakes out his hand, flexing his fingers. He looks at me again, his eyes pleading. "And now you really don't want me because I'm divorced. Damaged goods—"

I wince. "That's actually not true."

"—And worst of all, because I'm not Eric." His voice is raw. "You're afraid of real love, Vicky. You're too busy deluding yourself with the fantasy fluff you've built in your mind with a man who doesn't exist—"

"But Eric *is* a real man," I whisper.

"—to see the truth. You're afraid of imperfection.

That's why you're so obsessed with Eric; you see him as perfect. How could you ever be with someone who has flaws? What would people say? What would they think? You could never show your face in public with anyone who's less than perfect. Face it, Vicky. You're afraid of dirty dishwater and a man leaving the toilet seat up. Because where's the romance in that?"

"Fine! Is that what you want me to say, huh? Is that what you want me to admit? That there's nothing more in relationships than gross, ugly, snot-filled reality? That beauty doesn't exist and people who think that are hopelessly naïve and living in La-La Land? Who died and made you the boss of me, anyway? I'm the only one who's in charge of myself and what I believe. And besides, how dare you assume to know me that well!"

Now I'm crying, and my mascara is bleeding down my face. An oily, slimy feeling starts creeping inside me. Maybe I am pathetic. Filling my head with romantic nonsense. And for what reason, really? But those visions...

"Oh, Vicky, I'm sorry." He reaches out, traces a finger along my collarbone. "This is one of my big flaws." He swallows.

I start to speak but he runs a finger, feather-light, across the line of my neck for the briefest of moments, and I forget what I was about to say.

"Wanting to save people. Thinking I'm always right." There's sadness in his gaze. "Maybe I think that if I rescue you, I can see myself in a more heroic light." Now regret is in his eyes.

"Because I think that's what you're really looking for. A storybook hero." I see his jaw clench. "And

maybe, Vicky..." His voice is husky now, and he lifts my chin with a fingertip. "I have a desire to be your hero..."

I shiver. From the breeze or his touch, I'm not sure.

"Even if I've already made that mistake one time too many." His voice is low and his tone is anything but gentle. He drops his hand. "So I finally figured it out—I can't rescue you. You need to find the hero within yourself. I can't be with someone who's obsessed with a fantasy—while a real man is standing right in front of her. Because you don't want me, Vicky. You want the fantasy."

He turns and walks away.

Fine. Be like that. I stick my tongue out at his retreating back and spin around in the opposite direction, forgetting I'm standing in bare feet. On slippery tile.

By the time I realize I'm off balance, I'm already pitching forward. I try desperately to grab for something, anything, but there's only open air. My feet fly out from under me so fast I don't have time to scream as I crash onto the tile, hitting my head.

The only thought that flashes through my mind before everything goes black is, This is what I get for sticking my tongue out.

Chapter Fifteen

CAN'T MOVE. It feels like fire everywhere in my body. Am I in hell? Can't breathe. Can barely think. What's that weird beeping noise? *Beep. Beep. Beep.* Like one of those heart monitor things on *Grey's Anatomy* or *ER*. Hey, if this is hell, maybe George Clooney's on doctor duty.

My eyelids flutter at the thought and finally open, my vision slowly coming into focus. White room. White sheets. Metal machines. Yep. Not hell; a hospital.

"Awake, are you, sweetie?" I hear a rustle of clothing and catch a familiar whiff of *L'Air du Temps*.

"Mom?"

She lays a hand on my forehead, smoothing back my hair. "Your father and I were so worried. We got a phone call from someone named McCloud, and we flew straight out here. You were unconscious and the doctors thought…" She trails off, her eyes searching my face. "Well, never mind. The doctors were obviously wrong. But you need to take it easy, they said. A few bruised ribs, a strained wrist, and a mild concussion. Oh, and a bit of a sunburn."

Not to mention a bruised heart. I squeeze my eyes shut and fight off a wave of dizziness.

As I open them again, McCloud's words run through my head. *You need to find the hero within you.*

I have a choice about how I feel about this.

I look down at my bandaged torso. I choose...I choose *strength*. All at once, that exact feeling is coursing through me. Yes. I raise my chin. Strong. That's what I'm going to be.

I carefully sit up. "We can fly home?"

"Yes," my mom says.

❖ ❖ ❖

A WEEK LATER I'm settled back into the apartment I share with Cerise. I'm resting on the couch when I hear the jingle of keys in the lock.

"Hey," Cerise says. "Just checked the mail and this came for you."

I tear it open, my heart beating rapid-fire.

Vicky,

I wish things could've gone differently between us. But there's no rewind in life, I guess. I'm sorry about your accident. I hope you're feeling better now. I've enclosed the CD of your demo track. It turned out well. Nice to work with you and all the best.

Take care,
McCloud

❖ ❖ ❖

THE NEXT DAY, Cerise comes by for a visit. She settles onto the purple fluffy comforter, so at odds with her black Goth attire.

"Your mom told me what happened in Toronto."

I let out a sigh of relief. Then I frown and hand her McCloud's letter.

She reads it in silence before looking back up at me. "So what are you going to do about it?"

I pick at a piece of lint on the bedspread. "Nothing. I need to be strong. Move on. Obviously I can't handle anything more than fantasy." Suddenly I'm way too hot; I fling the covers back. "I pushed McCloud away—literally. For a made-up fantasy man." A small smile curls the corners of my mouth. "Leave it to me to do something like that. But there's something I just don't *get*. If the whole Eric thing was all a stupid crush, all made up, then why do I keep getting all these visions or whatever? And how does McCloud fit into it all? I mean, what was the universe trying to tell me?"

Cerise looks thoughtful.

My eyes widen. "Wait a second. I know exactly what I need to do to uncover the truth about this whole mess. Why didn't I think of it before? New Age is practically my middle name. Of course! I need to do a past life regression."

"I'll go get your CD," Cerise says.

A few minutes later, the mellow voice of the hypnotherapist on the self-hypnosis recording drifts through my mind as she counts backwards from twenty to one. I can feel myself relax more and more.

Down, down, down...*I find myself walking through a beautiful garden*. Down, down, down...*into a lovely meadow*. Down, down, down...*onto a sandy beach*. Down, down, down...*into my unconscious mind*. Going deeper and deeper and deeeeeeeper.

With that voice in my ear...telling me to enter a

dark cave at the edge of the beach, just enter the cave and walk to the light. Yes. Must walk to the light...the light...the light...

And now I'm stepping back, back, back in time...

I'm on the street. I'm wearing t-strap shoes of brown patent leather, with a sturdy heel and a rounded toe. Practical shoes that Mama bought for me on my last birthday. And there I am, standing on the big-city sidewalk, looking at a marvelous forest-green dress with the most darling little collar and black buttons...

But that doesn't matter so much, because now I hear someone telling me to move on to an important event in this lifetime. Oh yes. Yes. This is a regression, this isn't actually happening right now. It's only a memory.

Now it feels like I'm outside of the body of this young woman...who lives in Chicago... The year becomes clear in my mind. 1939. Yes. And this important event...

It's a year later. So terrible. So sad... I feel a weight on my chest. But this man George, this man is making me laugh and forget all my troubles, so I nod my head and say yes, yes I'll go with him to see a show. Yes. He's a good fellow, George. Handsome, too. Yes. Good of George to take me here, and he doesn't even know just how much I love jazz.

We sit down in the darkened club, the booth feels soft and slightly springy beneath me as I smooth out my skirt, glad I saved my best dress for tonight.

The curtain goes up on the small stage at the front of the small room. Oh George, I hear the most wonderful melody. A huge smile breaks out on my face. George smiles back, thinking I meant it for him.

But it's for the man onstage. He is...completely magi-

cal. His voice is like velvet, like satin, like rich cream.

George frowns. He's not fascinated. But he's a gentleman, and knows he has to wait till the show is over. So he leans toward me, offers me a light. I shake my head and he inhales on the dregs of his own cigarette.

Song after song. I'm completely entranced.

Before the final number, I slip into the powder room to touch up my lipstick. A persistent rapping at the door doesn't allow me the luxury of lingering. I dab at my lips, then swing the door open and let the next lady inside. The volume of voices around me tells me that the show has just concluded.

Intent on putting my lipstick back into my handbag while weaving my way between club-goers on my way back to George, I fumble with the clasp that always seemed to stick. Why did I bring this purse instead of my old reliable one? But I love this one's mother-of-pearl closure and shiny satin fabric, despite its tricky clasp. Finally I get the handbag open when I bump into someone, the sudden jolt sending the lipstick clattering to the floor.

"Oh, excuse me!" I look up and feel a thousand butterflies brush wings against my stomach. Such a strong flurry of joy surges through me that I'm breathless as our eyes meet.

It's him. It's him. Oh, it's him. My heart swells as wave upon wave of love pours through me. Yes, yes, oh yes. I see it in this man's eyes...his soul staring back at me through this man's intense gaze... My heart pounds faster, faster, faster. And I know exactly who he is— Eric Black. *And* Tom White.

"That's all right, miss." He holds up the lipstick tube and smiles at me. "I think you dropped this."

The scene shifts as I hear the hypnotherapist's voice say, "All right. Let's move on to the most significant event in this lifetime. You had a lot of important events happen to you in this life, but one is the most important. Let's go there right now..."

I'm looking down at the face of my baby daughter, wrapped in a blanket as I'm standing in the middle of the living room with my husband.

It's our apartment and we...our daughter...we got engaged last year and now, now we're married and we have Sadie, beautiful, beautiful darling baby Sadie. Tom slips an arm around my waist and he's so proud too, so happy and proud and full of awe.

We look down into our daughter's bright eyes. She's perfect. My eyes fill, my heart swells and there's such a powerful pull of love that I just let it wash over and through me, healing, cleansing. It's like something I've never known, yet known all along. Never experienced before until this very moment when I held this little person, this being of light, in my arms.

"All right. It's time to move on from this. Now I want you to see the most important person to you in this lifetime. Who had the most influence over you and who affected your life in the greatest, most important way?"

All at once, I'm standing in a train station, the inbound train from New York just pulling up. I'm waiting, and there, there he is! Overcoat buttoned, fedora in place, a huge grin on his face. Oh, he's so happy. Jubilant. He sweeps me up in his arms, spins me around in a circle and I'm breathless with laughter, breathless with joy.

He got the deal. He got the recording deal and oh, I'm so glad for him. He deserves it. His very first record.

He's going to be a real singer, with records to sell and dreams to come true and...our life together. He did it. And I'm so proud of him. I'll be right there with him, every step of the way.

Once again the scene shifts and I'm in our apartment, six months pregnant. In our bedroom. A piece of white catches my eye. Looks like a...a handkerchief, dainty sheer lace around the edges. Not like mine with crocheted edges. But I can't see all of it. Just that one little part. It has initials. No, those aren't Tom's initials. Those aren't my initials. Who... No. I'll wait till he gets home for dinner. He'll tell me then. I'm sure there's a logical explanation.

Tom's walking in, hanging up his hat, taking off his overcoat. Smiling. As if he doesn't even know. How could he? But I summon up the courage. Face him. Ask him. His face drops, his weight shifting from one foot to the other, a pleading note in his voice. She came over here. My ex-girlfriend. No, nothing happened.

He's speaking more quickly now, his hands in his trouser pockets. Now he's reaching for me, begging me to understand. I turn away. She dropped it, he says. Nothing happened, he says. She's always been the jealous type. And when, oh, darling, please, please listen to me. I love you. You. Not her. I never really did love her, not the way... Please understand. Please. I couldn't bear it if you... Please.

His arms slip around my waist but I pull back, clutching the wooden spoon. My only lifeline. This can't be happening. How could she just have dropped it? In the bedroom? No. It's impossible.

I don't believe you. You're lying to me. You're lying to me! You can't do this to me. After all I've done for you. I gave you everything and now you're treating me like this. How could you do this to me? I've been faithful. Loyal. Every moment of every hour of every day. Every heart-beat. Every second. And now our baby... I put a hand on my belly. No. No. No. I hate you. Get away from me. Don't touch me. Get out of here!

My voice rises, constricts. I'm choking, sobbing. No. Just leave. Leave me alone. I don't want to see you again. Ever.

No, sweetheart. No, no, no. Please. Darling. She couldn't stand it. She couldn't stand seeing us together and she came over one afternoon. Just listen. Listen to me. His grip is tightening on my arms.

I shake my head, trying to escape. His voice is too loud. Much too loud and insistent. His fingers dig into my arms. She cajoled her way in here. I told her to get out but she wouldn't listen. Just laughed in my face and slapped me. And then, then she left and I thought she hadn't left anything behind and I had to almost shove her out the door.

But she left. She left and I felt so relieved. It was yesterday. Please. I was going to tell you. I swear it. I swear to you on my life, on our baby's life, that nothing at all happened. She must have dropped it, planted it in the bedroom. She always hated my going out on tour, talking with other women. She couldn't stand it. Please, please. You have to believe me.

Just get out. Just get out!

And he does.

I scream, the sound ringing through the now dark and silent apartment. Tears, so many tears. I shake and sob, unable to control anything any longer, my heart beating so fast, so fast. Everyone has left, everyone has abandoned me. There's no reason, no reason at all to go on.

He cheated. I just know he did. After all I gave to him. All of it was for nothing. And now what is there to show for it? Nothing at all. I can't even think or speak or hear or move, but somehow I'm getting up, going into the kitchen. Our apartment is on the top floor. Tom was so proud of that. Well, Tom, what are you going to think of it now? Rage pours through me. How dare you, Tom. How dare you! You can't even begin to imagine how much I sacrificed for you.

I'm crossing the kitchen floor, moving to the window. Yes, ten floors up. Ten floors. Everything. I gave you my heart. My body. My soul. I meant those wedding vows. And you, you betrayed me!

A scream rips through me again and I heave the window open. Feel the cold rush of December air fill the room. Goose bumps raise on my skin. In a minute, it won't matter. None of it will matter anymore. And when I'm gone, he'll be sorry.

I lean out the window, the tears freezing to my face. I barely feel the damp. I lean further out but my belly... I touch my swollen stomach, my hand pressing against the distended skin through the gingham print fabric of my dress.

Tears pour down my face again. No. An icy knowing floods through me. The baby. I can't do this... I hang my head. I can't. I need to think of the baby. I have to live. For the baby. But there's...there's something else here too. I cock my head to the side as a burst of knowledge, a voiceless voice, flows through me, filling me, buoying me, protecting me.

All at once, I feel it. Yes. Yes. Hear the words: He's

telling the truth. *A warmth floods me, envelopes me, as if arms are surrounding me, protecting me, healing me, guiding me. And I know it to be true. Beyond the shadows of doubt and fear. Those words, encased in truth and light. The only thing that burns away the darkness.*

A peace and calm settle through me as my tears subside, my breathing slows, my heart rate returns to normal.

And once more, the scene shifts.

It's midnight. Darling, darling, Tom whispers, raining my face with kisses.

My apricot-colored slip falls to the floor. The dark wood headboard curves around us, the smooth cotton sheets cool beneath my warm skin.

The creak of the mattress beneath our combined weight. And oh, oh, oh, Tom's so tender, so gentle. So...reverent. His stubble brushes my cheek as he kisses my neck, my shoulder. Oh. I breathe in. He loves me. So much, so much. So sweet. So good. As much as I love him. My fingers twine themselves through his hair. I can't stand it. Oh God... Together. Together. Together.

We never were separate at all.

Now you will leave this past lifetime, the hypnotic voice intones. To let go. To understand what you learned because of it.

Oh, I don't want to hear this.

Not now, not when I'm discovering the hidden truth... But my mind, in such a state of relaxation, complies anyway, despite the fact that the smallest part of me wants to stay in these memories forever, these memories that seems so real, exquisite. Such a part of my heart...my soul.

The voice is calling again, guiding me to find, to understand, the truth behind all of this... What is the one biggest lesson you learned from this lifetime? A word or a phrase, a feeling or an emotion. All at once, the answer comes. *Trust and forgiveness.*

To trust. To make yourself vulnerable enough to have faith in the trust that had been extended, to trust in the realness of a deep, lasting relationship, for yourself, for everyone involved.

And forgiveness. Forgiveness for myself, and forgiveness for him, as well; forgiveness of everyone involved in the situation.

My lungs involuntarily inhale and exhale as if I'm breathing out, at last, all the fear and negativity and pain that I've been holding onto, that had been stored deep within my cells, deep within my subconscious, deep within my soul.

For wisdom erases karma, the voice intones, even as it guides me back, back, back, counting up from fifty to one, back to this body, this lifetime, this room, this moment.

My eyes slowly, slowly open. I take a deep breath, as if breathing for the very first time, as if the very act of taking in those particles of oxygen infuses within me a newness, a brightness and a lightness that didn't seem to exist before.

✦ ✦ ✦

I CAREFULLY SIT up, stretch, and pad to the kitchen for some blueberry tea. I wrap my hands around the mug, savoring the sense of peace that now resides within me. Because it all makes so much sense now.

Tom was Eric. Zosia was his ex. And George was McCloud. God, no wonder I was so messed up. New lifetimes, new bodies, new roles.

That's why I didn't recognize Eric as Tom right away in that dream I had, because at that point, I hadn't met either Eric or McCloud.

No wonder the roles reversed in this lifetime—that Zosia is with Eric now. No wonder I got so obsessed—because Eric was my husband. And no wonder McCloud and I got tangled up in our attraction to each other. We were all acting out those same old patterns. (Gotta love karma.)

I take my mug back to the kitchen and put it in the sink, grab the garbage and take it out to the red Dumpster in back of my apartment building. As I fling the bag of trash away, a surge of knowing pours through me. My relationship with Tom was a lighter kind of love. Light, sweet, delicate.

Even though Eric and I aren't together as a couple in this lifetime, that's okay. Because I get to keep the memories. It's necessary for me to learn something else now, to be with a man who understands me at an even deeper, core level, in this lifetime.

But have I found all this out too late?

❖ ❖ ❖

I HAVE TO try. So I hop a flight back to Toronto the next morning. I realize, as the airplane taxis and then takes off, that now that the little section of my heart labeled Eric Black is healed. I have plenty of room for acceptance.

I smile and take the drink the flight attendant

hands me. I don't have to reject that part of myself, I realize, which is what I'd been trying so hard to do, and why I'd been so filled with pain and terror this whole time. That's why I attracted my abusive ex, too. I let out a long sigh, my heart suddenly filled with a peace I didn't realize was missing.

I wheel my carry-on through the arrivals terminal in Toronto and step out into the bright Tuesday sunshine to hail a cab.

I can make room in my heart for a man who's actually there for me, actually present in my life. A man like...like...

"Where to, miss?" the cabbie asks.

"McCloud." I whisper his name and it seems to rise up above my head and float there, shimmering above me with an energy all its own, filled with the vibration of *us*—of me and McCloud—together.

"4656 89th Street West."

As the cab pulls away from the curb and merges with traffic, memories flash through my mind. McCloud strumming the guitar in the darkness, the naked vulnerability in his eyes; tending bar, working the sound equipment—competent, sexy, standing there by the pool, that tattoo, the strength of him, his neck, shoulders, chest, abs...

Our argument, when his eyes flashed green fire, burning so brightly I could see right into the depths of his soul.

Will he understand what I've come to know? The cab slows and pulls up to the door of the studio.

What if he rejects me? But no. It doesn't matter. Love is never wasted. Even if I never see him again. The vibrations of that love spread out, to enhance the whole world, the whole universe, in fact.

I get out of the cab.

And my book, I realize. My story was literally *my* story. *Lyrics of Love*—I wasn't inspired to write it. I was remembering my own lifetime. My past love. No wonder it flowed so easily.

I knock on the studio door as tears run down my face.

To jealously hoard all that love for one person, well, that's not love at all. That's fear. Thinking it only belongs to one person is utterly ridiculous. But I didn't know any better, so I can forgive myself, as well.

There's no answer. I knock again, undeterred.

In a way, this is about forgiveness, too. Love doesn't belong to any one person. It's a gift that keeps giving. It's our own makeup, our true nature, the blueprint of our souls.

Still no answer. I straighten my spine, take out my phone and dial the studio number. It rings.

That's what Eric showed me, in this lifetime—he was a representation, a roadmap, a guidepost to my own relationship with the right man, who's not perfect, but who's perfect for me. (Trust me, I know the difference now.)

I thought I had to have Eric or nothing. But it doesn't work that way. Because love is a position of power, not of weakness. Love is the ultimate power.

He's not picking up.

And because of that ultimate power, I can be strong enough to accept McCloud's humanity, his vulnerability, every aspect of him and all his qualities without fear. Without running away. Love accepts everyone and everything for what and who they are, without judgment or cruelty or...withholding.

I wince, remembering our final argument. Love has grace and power and beauty and elegance.

I lift my chin and put away my phone. Well, there's only one other choice. I'm going to his condo.

Chapter Sixteen

THE CAB PULLS up to the entrance of McCloud's building. I get out, walk up the steps and over to the concierge desk. "Can I help you?"

"Yes. Is McCloud Xavier in?" I tap my fingers as the concierge buzzes him.

Those fears; they were all excuses, I realize. Those lies; they were all fake.

McCloud knew that. He knew that all along.

Perhaps he was more perfect for me than I could've ever thought. Because Eric, and my ex, they didn't know me. I didn't know them. I barely knew myself. I know me better, now. And McCloud knows me pretty dang well, too.

"I'm sorry, miss. He's gone."

"Gone as in out for the afternoon?"

"Gone as in he packed his bags and left."

"He didn't say where he was going or...anything?"

"No."

✧　✧　✧

SO THAT'S HOW this thing ends? The moment I have all these awesome epiphanies, the moment I have my heart open, is the moment everything goes poof.

I get back into the cab. Whatever. No, I won't be bitter.

As the cab weaves through lanes of traffic heading toward the airport, I lift my chin. Time for a little pick-me-up. I whip out my compact.

I apply glitter eye shadow to one lid, then swipe the shadow across my other lid. My mind, of course, flicks back through the memories like a montage— McCloud and me laughing on the motorcycle, us kissing, him shaking my hand when we first met. That gleam in his eyes; the way he looked at me when I told him about my story; how he held me when I was so selfishly bawling about Eric and his wife.

I stare at myself in the small circular mirror for a long moment without blinking. Hmmm, I should use this shade more often.

Then I look. Really look.

And I see her. Her. The real me. The woman that exists beyond all my perceptions and all my fears.

I stare back at the strong, beautiful woman who regards me with such a sense of surety. Yes. She doesn't have walls or barriers to conveniently hide behind. She's not allowing herself the false luxury of pretense and pretending.

She knows there never were any barriers to love in the first place. She knows that these are all illusions that I've put up within my heart to protect me from...what?

From joy? From gladness? From delight? From the vulnerability of heartbreak?

God. I've been so stupid.

The woman in my mirror smiles. No, not stupid. Just human.

❖   ❖   ❖

I SETTLE INTO my seat at the gate and pull out the gift I'd planned to give McCloud and run a hand across it—a Buddy Holly memoir—and feel so sad. As I put the book away, I know that even though my feelings for McCloud are still strong, my art will help me get over this, just like art had gotten me into this in the first place... Art is my refuge and my saving grace. It lies within myself and relies upon no one but me.

As the flight begins boarding and I walk down the jet bridge to the plane, the toe of my shoe nudges a few crumpled gum wrappers and the scent of stale coffee wafts over me, but this only brings me comfort.

Because it means life goes on. It means that I can express my feelings to McCloud if only through the words of my art. (And while I'm at it, I'll email him, just for closure.) It doesn't even matter whether he ever reads any of it, either. The sole act of me writing the message gives it all the shape, meaning and validation it needs. I pull out my phone and start typing.

✧　　✧　　✧

BACK IN REGINA at last. I don't think I want to see the inside of another airplane—or airport—for a long time. Maybe ever. I'll start taking the bus everywhere. Or the train.

I walk slowly down the sidewalk, savoring my newfound freedom, barely registering the poufy-haired old lady walking her dogs down the street, or the sweaty shirtless middle-aged jogger in his velour pants.

Or the guy in jeans and a T-shirt, with a half-day's

growth of stubble, leaning against the column beside the entryway to my apartment building.

Yep, just my regular neighborhood... I do a double-take as I walk up the steps.

The guy moves toward me. Now he's close enough to touch. So I do, his familiar Ivory soap and clean laundry scent filling me.

"You're not making me up, Vicky," McCloud whispers. "I'm real." He reaches out to take my hand. "Come with me."

"Wait. We owe each other about a hundred explanations...and where are we going? How did you find out where I live?"

"I found your address in the phone book. We'll have plenty of time to talk when we get where we're going. It's a good place that I think you just might like." He winks.

My heart flutters as his palm slides against mine and our fingers interlace.

He enters my apartment building and walks to the end of the hallway, then takes out a key from his back pocket and fits it into the lock. The door swings open.

"This is really sweet of you and all, but just a second. Where'd you get the key?"

"Turns out your landlord's a romantic." He grins. "And I gave her my cell phone for collateral."

"Oh. But wait. I thought you said you couldn't be with someone who was obsessed with a fantasy?"

"That hasn't changed. The thing is, I've had time to think. I was on a business trip in Vancouver when I got your cryptic email. By then, I'd already decided to come. Some of your impulsiveness must have rubbed off on me, because I decided to chance coming to

Regina. I wanted to talk to you in person. So." He turns and holds the door open for me, making a sweeping gesture with his free arm. "Ladies first."

"Look at you, being Mr. Gallant."

He bows. "Anything to win m'lady's favor."

I laugh.

It catches in my throat when I step through the doorway and am confronted by a metal ladder affixed to the wall that reaches up. Way up. "Uhhh..."

"Oh. Are you afraid of heights?" A concerned line forms on his forehead. "Because, uh," he chuckles nervously, "I didn't think of that."

"Actually, no. I'm not." I gesture to my pink polka dot dress. I just don't want him to be staring up my skirt if I'm the first one to go up the ladder.

"I'll go first."

I blush. "Thanks."

We reach the top of the ladder and there's another, smaller door which McCloud opens with yet another key.

"You have almost as many keys as Quasimodo." I give him a playful dig in the ribs, which causes him to almost drop them. "Oops. Sorry about that."

He laughs. "It's okay." He turns his attention back to the door and it swings open, revealing our destination.

The roof.

He steps out onto the flat roof, then extends his hand to me. "Careful. There's a bit of a ledge there."

I refuse his hand and take a deep breath. It's now or never. "You know how you said I was living in my head, with all that fantasy and no reality, obsessed with thinking I had to be with Eric?"

He tenses. "Yeah."

"Well, it turns out we were all mixed up together in a past life. The four of us—Eric, Zosia, you, me. And Eric was my husband back then."

He whistles, long and low. "Looks like I was wrong about a lot of things," he says quietly. "I'm sorry if I hurt you. Past lives, huh?" He studies the skyline.

The silence seems to stretch forever.

Finally, he turns back to me. "There's so much to this world if you look beyond the surface. It makes sense, actually." His eyes are an intense emerald. "A chance to get things right, then, this time around." He smiles. Extends his hand again.

I take his outstretched hand and step gingerly across the threshold.

Still holding hands, we cross to the center of the roof. I look around, holding my breath. The view is absolutely spectacular. Lights twinkle all around us in the near-darkness.

"Do you see what I see?"

"A view of the city at dusk?"

"That too." McCloud's lips quirk up into a smile as he trails a finger down my cheek. "What I see..." His voice gets husky. "Is the truth. The truth that's standing right here. Right now. In *this* lifetime." His breath fans my face and I hear him swallow, his voice coming out even lower, reverberating through me.

"The truth that I couldn't see before because my ex-wife..." He clenches his jaw. "She was a singer, and we had a really unhealthy relationship that brainwashed me into thinking that I..." He shakes his head. "That I could never share an artistic relationship with anyone that went beyond the sound booth. That's why I was so hesitant to make a move on you for so long. And like I told you at Eric's, I have this whole pattern of wanting to save people. Which is why I thought I had to walk away from you. But I used your obsession with Eric as an excuse to cover my own fears.

"I thought you expected me to save you, too. That's what my ex-wife was looking for. When we moved in together, it got worse instead of better. I don't know why I thought it would get easier when we got married. And then when we got divorced, I felt so guilty for feeling so relieved. I just thought that it'd be better never to do anything like that again with an artist."

I blink once, twice, three times. "I-I can't be with you, then." Even though I'm falling for him.

"No, Vicky." He slides an arm around my waist. "I thought I couldn't be with you. Oh God," McCloud groans. "I was an idiot to ever let you get away. Why did I think that it wouldn't work between us, that my heart couldn't take any more? Well, screw that. Because I'm starting to fall in love with you."

I stare at him, openmouthed. "But how? I mean, you live in Toronto. And I live in Regina. I'm starting to fall in love with you too, but I don't know how to— I mean, I've never been in love before and I don't want to burden you or—"

"Don't worry about how. We'll figure it out together." When he pulls me to him this time, I thread my fingers through his hair and let myself melt into the moment. There's nothing to prepare. Nothing to get right. Nothing to get wrong, either.

Love is never a burden. Because it's love. *It always helps. It never hurts. Only fear does that.*

"Besides, I like Regina. I could really do some great things for the music scene here. Plus, I'll have more time to shop your song around to artists. Who knows? Maybe Miss Swift would even record it." McCloud brushes a stray curl off my forehead. "Oh, and there's something else." He reaches into his pocket and pulls out an envelope. "I called 13 Management. Turns out Taylor's in a music video shoot right now in Prague, so she couldn't come by for cupcakes. But..."

He hands the envelope to me. "Voilà."

I take it from him and open the flap. Two pieces of shiny, glossy paper are tucked inside.

I let out a squeal. "Taylor Swift meet and greet tickets for her upcoming perfume launch!" I jump up and down. "*Thankyouthankyouthankyou!*"

"You're very welcome."

"I have something for you, too." I hand him the book.

He twines one of my curls around his finger. "Thank you."

"Guess what else?"

"What else?"

"Even though my novel wasn't published, I've decided to combine the book, plus everything that's happened, and write about this whole experience." I glance shyly at him. "I'm going to self-publish it. And I already have a title picked out."

"Oh yeah? That's great. What is it called?"

"You mean you don't know?" I bat my lashes at him.

He laughs. "Enlighten me."

"*Love, Your Fangirl.*"

A slow grin spreads across his face and he tugs me to him for another kiss. I welcome it, and I welcome him. He puts his arms around me and I relish the sense of safety and security that envelopes me. Warm and strong and sure. I relax into his warmth, his strength, his secure embrace. Because I can be safe in his arms at last.

Thanks for reading!

If you enjoyed *Love, Your Fangirl*, find more stories by Jessica Eissfeldt at your local bookseller or online retailer or visit jessicaeissfeldt.com.

Acknowledgments

Thank you to my writing group for moral support, as well as to my editor, Heather Obsorne, my proofreader Shannon Page and my cover designer, Angela Waters.